SPANISH GOLD

T0040397

SPANISH GOLD

GOLD

KEVIN RANDLE

M. EVANS
Lanham • Boulder • New York • Toronto • Plymouth, UK

Published by M. Evans
An imprint of Rowman & Littlefield
4501 Forbes Boulevard, Suite 200, Lanham, Maryland 20706
www.rowman.com

10 Thornbury Road, Plymouth PL6 7PP, United Kingdom

Distributed by National Book Network

Copyright © 1990 by Kevin D. Randle
First paperback edition 2014

All rights reserved. No part of this book may be reproduced in any form or
by any electronic or mechanical means, including information storage and
retrieval systems, without written permission from the publisher, except
by a reviewer who may quote passages in a review.

British Library Cataloguing in Publication Information Available

Library of Congress Cataloging-in-Publication Data

The hardback edition of this book was previously cataloged by the Library of
Congress as follows:

Randle, Kevin D., 1949-
    Spanish Gold / Kevin D. Randle
        p. cm.—(An Evans novel of the West)
    I. Title. II. Series.
    PS3568.A534S64   1990   90-42202
    813'.54—dc20

ISBN: 978-1-59077-237-9 (pbk. : alk. paper)
ISBN: 978-1-59077-238-6 (electronic)

∞™ The paper used in this publication meets the minimum requirements of
American National Standard for Information Sciences—Permanence of
Paper for Printed Library Materials, ANSI/NISO Z39.48-1992.

Printed in the United States of America

Chapter One
New Spain
July, 1692

It was a miserable country, this New World, filled with heathens, serpents, and savages. An arid, baking landscape that sucked the strength from men, killing the unwary in hours.

Capitano Pablo Alverez climbed from the back of his horse and slipped down the bank of a shallow river until he stood ankle deep in the water. He was a short man, his black hair long and his beard flowing. He wore a silver chest protector, a metal helmet, and leather boots. The armor had been brought from the Old World and the boots had been hand-tooled in the New. Pulling off a glove, he bent, dipped his hand into the water, and tasted it.

"Muddy," he said.

The caravan halted on the dusty banks behind him. Across the river, a hundred yards away, was a rocky cliff that climbed into the deep blue of the afternoon sky. There were trees, the green leaves fluttering in the breeze, bushes that rattled like the snakes that were everywhere, and a soft sand. The river itself had a reddish color, the dirt washed down by rains the day before looking like the lifeblood of an empire flowing away.

It was as hot as any of them ever remembered. All were sweating under the layers of clothing and armor meant to protect them from the savages that inhabited the hellhole. The long, never-ending ride hadn't helped, and the burden they guarded didn't lighten the journey.

"Horses first," ordered Alverez. Again he dipped his hand, but this time he wiped the water on his face trying to cool his body. "A thoroughly miserable country."

The horsemen walked their beasts to the river and allowed them to drink. Slaves, taken from the villages that had been plundered in New Spain, carried water to the horses hitched to wagons and carts while the infantry stood guard.

"A month," said Alverez. "A month and we'll be on the ships home."

"With enough treasure to buy anything we desire," said another. He was younger, taller, and the brother of the first.

"Cortez had the same but fell from grace. Treasure does not assure position."

The younger Alverez took a deep breath and then dropped to his knees. He washed his face in the stream, standing a moment later. "Cortez was a fool."

Turning, Alverez looked back at the caravan. A hundred men from Spain and two hundred natives. Horses brought at great expense from the Old World, wagons built in Mexico and driven northward into the desert. Pennants flew from some. Colored flags from others. Food had been found along the trail. Meat taken from the huge herds of antelope that jumped across the prairie. All of that now stopped along the bank of a river ankle deep and a mile across.

"Camp here tonight?"

"No. We have several more hours of sun."

"The men are tired. The horses are tired. A rest here would make tomorrow easier."

"If we press on, then we'll be home that much sooner. There is no reason to stay the night."

In the distance, at the end of the caravan, a horse reared and whined. A man fought to calm it. Soldiers who had lined the river turned, suddenly nervous. The slaves pulled back toward the wagons.

"What?" asked Alverez.

A soldier ran toward him. He stopped short and wiped a hand over his sweat-covered face. Pointing to the rear, where a cloud of dust was rising, he said, "Something comes."

"Skirmishers out," ordered Alverez. "Throw up a line at the end of the column." Alverez leaped up onto the bank, slipped in the sand, and scrambled up.

2

"Jose, get the Indians back along the river. Four men to watch them. They move, kill them."

"Certainly Pablo."

Two men ran toward the end of the caravan. One climbed up on the rear of a wagon to stare into the distance. The sunlight reflecting off the sand made it difficult to see more than a few feet. Light shrubbery, small plants with only a few leaves, concealed the base of the dust cloud.

Alverez ran toward the right. "Pull the wagons around to form a barricade and then unfasten the horses."

A half dozen men jumped forward. One grabbed the reins to pull the lead wagon until it was on the bank. The others followed suit forming a half moon using the river as a base.

With his brother, Alverez ran toward the Indian slaves. He leaned down, yanked a man to his feet and demanded, "What is happening?"

The Indian shrugged and in poor Spanish answered, "I know not."

"Who's coming?"

"No one."

Alverez cocked his fist and slammed it forward into the Indian's face. He heard bones snap as the nose flattened. Blood splattered down the Indian's bare chest and silently dripped to the sand.

Pointing a finger at the slaves huddled on the bank, he demanded, "What is happening?"

The Indians ignored him.

The lookout leaped from the rear of the wagon and ran toward Alverez. "Horsemen come."

"How many?"

"I couldn't tell. Maybe fifty or a hundred."

Alverez wiped a hand over his face. Sweat dripped and his breathing was now labored. He knew who it had to be. The Indians were coming after them to steal the gold and free the slaves.

"I want the skirmishers to fall back into the defensive perimeter. We do not let the enemy get close. Firearms first and then crossbows."

The soldier nodded and whirled to obey the order.

"Martinez," said Alverez, "take three men out as pickets."

Before he could answer, his neck spurted blood and a shaft grew from it. He reached up to finger his throat and then collapsed forward, falling on his face. Blood spread around him, soaking into the sand.

Alverez dropped to one knee, a flintlock pistol in his hand. He turned toward a copse of trees fifty yards away, but there was no one hiding there. "Anyone see where that came from?"

Before anyone could answer, another arrow flashed, slamming into the side of the wagon with a thud. A second followed the first, and then the air was filled with them. They buried themselves in the hard wood of the wagons, the soft sand under them, and the bodies of the horses which screamed in pain and fear.

"Behind us," yelled a soldier. He stood and ran to the river bank, sliding down to the edge of the water. "They're coming up behind us."

But there was no one visible behind them. The opposite bank was two or three feet high and covered with bushes and trees. Behind it the land was flat. No cover for the attacking savages. Yet the arrows kept coming, dropping among the skirmishers. A man was hit and toppled into the water with a large splash. A second fell back, screaming in pain.

"Fire," ordered Alverez. "Fire!"

There was a rattling of weapons. Clouds of blue-gray smoke billowed outward and then drifted on the light breeze. A quick volley into the trees opposite them and then momentary silence.

From all around them came a whooping. First a single voice and then another and another until it seemed that the woods were alive with beasts. The first of the enemy appeared. Huge men dressed in nothing but paint. They dashed forward toward the wagons, and then suddenly retreated, fleeing for cover.

"Kill them now!" yelled Alverez. "Kill them all."

Arrows from the crossbows flashed. One of the attackers took a bolt in the back. He fell to the river bank opposite them, and rolled down into the water.

The Spaniards scrambled to reload the rifles. There was shouting along the line. Two of the horses broke from the circle, leaped a gap between the wagons, and galloped away. One of the Indian slaves tried to escape but was shot, sprawling on the sand. No one moved to the body.

"Steady!" yelled Alverez. "Steady."

And then the Indians attacked. First a few leaping into the river, running in the ankle deep water, followed by more and more until it seemed that the bank was alive with the enemy. A shrieking, screaming horde, rushing forward, threatening to overrun the Spanish line.

"Coming up behind us," yelled a man. "There are more behind us." His voice had risen, filled with panic.

Alverez stood and turned, running to a wagon. He reached up, touched the side, and saw another force attacking them, these men mounted on horses. Fifty of them. Maybe more.

As he watched, the pickets deserted their posts, running for the safety of the wagons, but the horsemen caught them. Using clubs and lances and knives, the Indians cut down the fleeing men. Savages leaped from the horses, cutting, slashing, stabbing at the three dying men.

The main body of attackers did not stop. They rode on, whooping and screaming. Alverez glanced to the rear, then forward, and in that moment, didn't know what to do. The Indians were all around him.

"Fire!" he screamed.

There was a single volley. Smoke from the weapons rolled out over the river. A few of the attackers fell but the others came on, angered. They didn't slow as the crossbow bolts began to fly. More dropped into the shallow water, blood beginning to stain it.

Alverez held his ground, turning so that his right side was toward the oncoming enemy. He aimed his pistol carefully, bringing his hand down in the classic technique. He squeeze the trigger, saw the spark flash, and heard the weapon fire. The target was lost in a cloud of blue smoke that burst from the barrel.

He whirled at a sound behind him. The riders had reached the wagons. He drew his sword and stepped back, away from the makeshift wall so that he would be able to maneuver. Around him the two forces met with a sound like the surf on a beach. A sudden crash. Steel clanging against the stone of lances and the hardwood of the clubs. Men grunted and screamed and cried out. There were wet slaps and piercing shrieks of agony as both defender and attacker died.

An Indian warrior who was nearly nude and carrying a lance attacked a Spanish soldier in armor and leather and using a sword of the finest Toledo steel. The soldier slashed, hacking an arm from the Indian and then driving the blade into the attacker's chest. The Indian staggered to the rear, holding his wound as blood poured from it.

The soldier died an instant later, a lance shoved into the small of his back from behind. He screamed in surprise, falling forward onto his sword.

An Indian attacked Alverez. His face was painted in black and white, giving him the look of a skull that grinned. Alverez lunged and the savage leaped rearward. He slashed to the right and the attacker tried to dance away. The tip of the blade cut his bare belly, drawing a bloody line across it. The surprised man dodged in the wrong direction and Alverez killed him with a sudden lunge.

Alverez whirled, his back against the side of a wagon, and realized that his men were dying too fast. Their bodies were scattered along the bank and behind the line of wagons. Most of the horses had been driven off, and the slaves had grabbed weapons dropped by the dead and turned them on the defenders. The war whoops mixed with the cries of the wounded and the dying filled the air.

The attackers were killing the wounded, smashing heads with clubs or cutting throats with stone knives. They set fire to the wagons. Smoke filled the air as they looted the caravan, carrying off the food, the clothes, and the gold that had been taken from the mines to the west.

Alverez knew that all was lost. His brother was dead. The majority of his men were dead and the rest were dying at the hands of the whooping, screaming savages. He whirled, leaped between two wagons, thrust at an Indian, and then ran. Ran as fast as he could, not looking back. Not caring what was happening behind him. He ran away from the scene of the massacre. Away from the celebrating Indians and the burning wagons. He fell once, and then crawled forward into an arroyo, the side sloped and the dirt hard, almost like stone.

Scrambling around, he saw that the Indians were swarming all over the wagon train. They were wearing the armored chest plates and the helmets of dead soldiers. They were dancing with the heads of his soldiers decorating the tips of their lances. They were waving the pennants and flags they captured. And a few of them were carrying the bars of gold across the river and toward the bluffs in the distance.

Having caught his breath, Alverez glanced to the left. The arroyo narrowed, but offered him some protection. He pushed himself away from the sides, slid to the bottom, and began running along it. After a while he could no longer hear the screams of his men or smell the smoke of the burning wagons. A while longer, and he no longer heard the celebration chants of the dancing savages.

Chapter Two
Gettysburg
July, 1863

The cannonade had begun just after noon and had not let up for hours. Explosions erupted in the Union lines, ripping at the men and the equipment. The Federal batteries, dug in on the top of Cemetery Ridge, returned fire, matching the Rebels round for round until the barrels began to glow a dull cherry and the powder reserves ran low.

David Travis, a young man who had been swept up with passion after the Confederate victory at Bull Run and had joined the army, now crouched behind a split-rail fence. He had shed his blue coat in the afternoon heat and watched as the artillerymen fired volley after volley at the Rebel lines.

Travis was surrounded by thousands of other soldiers. Some, like him, had seen horror after horror. They had watched friends ripped to pieces by artillery or shot to pieces by rifle volley, or hacked to bits in the hand-to-hand fighting that often followed the first few shots.

Travis, his head down so that he couldn't see the Confederate cannons opposite him on Seminary Ridge, waited for the attack he knew was coming. For three days the men had maneuvered, fought, and died on that ground. Thousands had been killed and thousands more had been wounded. During the nights, when the winds died and the shooting slowed, the cries of the wounded and dying drifted over the battlefield and toward Gettysburg.

"They're coming!" screamed a man. He stood up and pointed, looking back at the Union lines.

An officer ran forward and took a position near the Angle. He wore a black hat and a dirty blue uniform. In one hand he held a pistol and in the other, a sword.

"Prepare to fire," he ordered.

Travis looked up then. The shadow valley in front of him was filled with smoke and dust. The booming of the artillery, sounding like the thunder of a distant storm, faded slowly. In the trees opposite them the first of the long gray lines of enemy soldiers appeared.

"Hold your fire," screamed the officer and the order was passed along the line. "Hold your fire."

"Wait for them to get into range."

"Pick your targets. Make every shot count."

Travis wiped his face on the red flannel sleeve of his sweat-stained shirt. He took a deep breath and swallowed the lump in his throat, suddenly afraid.

From the right, five hundred yards away, came a rattling of weapons. Clouds of light blue smoke rolled out as one brigade opened fire. The volley slammed into the left flank of the attacking Rebel divisions. Men fell, dead or wounded. Others pressed forward, filling in the gaps as they struggled to maintain straight lines.

"Hold your fire," ordered the officer close to Travis. "Wait for it."

There was a rippling of fire from the far left. The artillery fell silent and the drifting smoke obscured the ground in front of them. Another volley from the right smashed into the Confederates and one regiment broke, turning to run. But the others kept marching forward, their lines as straight as those on a parade ground.

All at once there was a scream from the Rebels and then a surging charge. The three divisions that Pickett commanded merged into a single mass of men that seemed to be guiding on a single copse of trees just behind Travis. To him it looked as if the entire Confederate army was attacking him personally.

"Take them," ordered the officer. "TAKE THEM!"

Travis lifted his rifle and aimed into the center of the attacking mass. As he pulled the trigger, a thousand others did the same thing. There was single, drawn-out crash as the weapons fired and a rolling, boiling blue cloud of gunsmoke.

A hundred, two hundred Rebel soldiers died in seconds. The attackers were engulfed in a cloud of smoke and fire. Bits of bodies exploded upward. Equipment flew apart. There were screams of pain and shrieks of agony.

And then there was a shout from the Rebels. A single, long cry made up from ten thousand soldiers as they suddenly rushed the Union lines. A moment later, as the Federals struggled to reload their rifles, the two forces crashed into one another. The fighting became hand-to-hand as the two sides mixed.

The smoke from the cannon and the rifles and muskets filled the air, hiding and then revealing the soldiers. The sun faded and the landscape turned gray. The world was suddenly locked in twilight where the ghostly shapes of men struggled to kill each other. The fighting was bayonet against bayonet, pistol against pistol, and man against man.

Travis tossed his useless rifle to the side and drew his revolver, searching for a target in the smoke. A single, hatless Rebel loomed over him, climbing to the top of the fence, but before he could move, Travis shot him in the stomach. Blood splattered back, splashing Travis. The odor of gunpowder was overwhelmed by that of hot copper and human bowel. The man wailed as he wrapped both hands around his belly and toppled back off the fence.

"Kill them all!" screamed the officer.

"Help me!" shrieked a man.

Travis turned toward the sound of the voice. A Rebel soldier held the barrel of his own weapon, the bayonet on the end of it, and tried to stab a wounded Yankee soldier. Travis aimed, fired, and saw the Rebel's head explode into a crimson cloud.

Travis felt something smash into his side. He staggered to the right and fell, rolling on his back. The Rebel soldier stood over him, his weapon held in both hands, the steel bayonet pointed at his chest. Travis fired once, twice, three times, and the enemy fell back.

The Rebels surged forward, screaming, overrunning a Union battery. They pushed beyond that, toward Meade's headquarters on the ridge, shouting their victory.

But the Union counterattacked, throwing another regiment into the fight. More men died, some quickly, a bullet in the head or the heart. Others fell wounded, their blood pumping from them to turn the ground into a bloody quagmire.

Travis was suddenly lost in a twilight world. Everything faded, disappearing in the drifting clouds of dust and smoke. The shouts, screams, and orders were lost as he stood, his empty pistol in his hand.

Something came at him. A deformed man. One arm was missing and the side of his uniform was soaked in blood. His face was white and he dragged his rifle behind him. Travis watched as the man stopped, looking skyward, and then toppled forward, landing on his face. In that moment, the Rebel attack broke. There never was any command to retreat. Just too many soldiers who had taken too much. Given too much. They turned from the Angle, from the split-rail fence, from the Union lines, and began the long, slow march back to Seminary Ridge.

All around him the Yankees poured fire into the retreating mass. Volley after volley slashed at the Rebels, killing more of them. The men dropped in piles, their bodies littering the open ground.

Cannon on the ridge behind the Yankees fired down into the valley, slaughtering the survivors. Hundreds were killed in the retreat.

"Cease fire. Cease fire. Cease fire."

But the men refused to obey the order, loading their weapons and firing at the fleeing Rebels. Some were screaming their hatred. Others stood numbly, looking at the broken bodies of the dead scattered on the open ground.

Travis stood silently behind the split-rail fence, his empty revolver in his hand. The odor of death drifted to him, overwhelming the gunpowder. He was afraid to breathe, afraid to move.

Around him the firing tapered and died. Those who hadn't been wounded in the fight, stood, one by one, facing the open ground where Pickett's and Pettigrew's divisions had been cut to ribbons. An unhealthy silence descended, punctuated by the booming of the artillery and the cries of the wounded.

"Jesus," said a man, his voice low. "Jesus."

An officer mounted on a huge brown horse galloped up. He reined it to a halt in a cloud of dust and looked down at a lieutenant who stood hatless.

"I want you to get your men moving. We're going to counterattack."

"Sir?"

"You heard me. Get ready to attack." He jerked on the reins and the horse turned. He galloped off.

The lieutenant glanced at the men who were standing silently. Dirty, sweaty men with vacant eyes. Men who, for the moment, had lost the ability to reason, and the lieutenant knew that he could never get them to attack the Confederate positions.

Travis waited for orders. Sergeants moved along the line, checking the bodies of the dead and treating the wounded. Stretcher-bearers walked the field searching for the injured, loading them and rushing to the rear where the field hospitals stood.

Everyone else was numb. The shock of battle had not worn off. The scene of horror that stretched in front of them had not sunk in. They were men who had survived an hour of total terror and could no longer think.

One man sat on the ground, his head resting against the bottom rail of the fence, his shoulders shaking as he cried. Another stood, his face pale, streaked with dirt and grime, and mumbled a single, unintelligible word over and over again.

Travis slowly came out of his trance. The odors, the sights, the sounds beat against him like the rain of a thunderstorm. He glanced down at his pistol and then at the man who lay dead at his feet.

"I've got to get out," he said.

"What?"

Travis looked at the man standing beside him and shook his head. He holstered his pistol and moved away from the fence. He turned, looking up toward the crest of Cemetery Ridge where there were thousands of soldiers, tents, cannon, horses, wagons, and rows of wounded.

"I've got to get out," he mumbled. He began to climb the hill, slowly at first, and then faster and faster until he was running upward.

At the crest, standing among the officers who had watched the attack and with the pale-faced men sickened by the butcher's yard in front of them, Travis turned. Below him was a sight that he knew he'd never forget. Below him was a scene that he hoped he would never see again.

Chapter Three
Sweetwater, Texas
August 6, 1863

Travis was leaning on the bar made from two thick planks set on top of barrels. In front of him was a bottle of warm whiskey and a thickset man in sweat-stained clothes and slicked-back hair. There was a scar from his right eye down to his chin that looked to be no more than a few months old. Three fingers of his right hand were missing.

"Happened at Manassas," said the bartender. He held up the hand and then fingered his scar. "Yankee did it. I killed the bastard."

Travis kept his eyes on the whiskey and didn't respond.

"Haven't seen you around here before," said the bartender quietly.

"That a problem?"

"Nope. Just wondering why you're not back east in the fighting."

"Maybe I got tired of it," said Travis. He cupped the shot glass so that it was difficult to see. He stared down into the liquor.

"So you fought?"

"You ask a lot of questions," said Travis.

"Just trying to be friendly."

Travis didn't respond.

Two men pushed through the half-doors. Both were covered with trail dust and sweat. One of them pulled his hat off, wiped his forehead and then shouted, "Whiskey."

The other stood silhouetted in the door and stared at Travis, looking him up and down like a boxer studying his opponent. Finally he pushed on through and stepped up to the bar, next to his partner.

Travis drained his glass and glanced out the doorway because the windows were opaque, greased paper that only let in the light. Travis thought about leaving now that the other two men had arrived, but decided against it. The fact they wore gray trousers that resembled those of the Rebel army had not been lost on him.

"You boys from?" asked the bartender.

"Kansas. Up there with the raiders but decided to get out for a while. Things to do down here." One of them glanced over at Travis and then raised his drink.

Travis turned back to the bar and snagged the bottle from it, pouring himself another drink. The bartender moved toward him until Travis dropped a coin on the planks. Smiling, the bartender retreated, standing next to the wooden wall near the two newcomers.

The saloon was shabby. Rough, dirty planks for the floor, two tables against one wall, and a half dozen chairs and two stools. A hot, dry wind blew in the open door and a fly buzzed around a wet spot on the bar.

They all drank in silence with the bartender making sure that no one took a shot without paying for it. One of the Kansans looked toward Travis but said nothing.

A shadow fell across the door and an old man appeared. He stood there, the bright sunlight behind him making it impossible to see him. He pushed in, limped slowly to the bar. "Need a drink."

"You got money?"

The old man shrugged. "Not with me."

"Then get out."

The old man leaned forward and lowered his voice. "I got something better than money. Something that could provide you with all the money you could ever want. More money than you could dream about."

The man was dressed in worn, frayed jeans, a flannel shirt that was threadbare and filthy. His hair was graying and dirty, and his beard was crusted and brushed his chest. He dropped his hat, a beat-up, shapeless black thing, on the bar.

"I could tell you a story," he said.

"Beat it old man," said the bartender.

"No," said one of the Kansans. He threw a coin on the bar. "Give the man a drink and let him tell us about all the money we could imagine."

"Thank you," he said.

Travis turned away from them, not wanting to listen. He knew from the sound of the voices that the men were baiting the old prospector. They were bored and amusing themselves, and he didn't want to watch.

"You won't be sorry." He waited for the bartender to give him a drink, lifted it to his lips, and tasted it. "The nectar of the gods," he said.

"The money old man. The money."

"Not money. Gold. Bars of it. Hundreds of bars of it. Hidden in a cave."

"Bull."

The old prospector finished his drink. "Another?" He glanced at the two Kansans.

"Not for a cock and bull story of gold bars in a cave."

"I saw them. Got a map."

"Let's see the map," said one of them moving closer.

"Nope. It's my secret."

"You said that you'd tell us where all this gold was."

"Nope. I said I'd tell you a story about all the gold you could imagine. Bars of it stacked on the floor of a cave. Dust covers gold so it looks gray like lead but it's gold. Hundreds of bars of it."

"Where'd it come from?"

The prospector pointed at his empty glass.

"Give him another drink."

Travis picked up his glass and moved back to one of the tables. He sat down and tried not to listen to the story.

"Spanish gold," said the prospector when the bartender filled his glass. "Mined in New Mexico or Arizona a long time ago. They was transporting it to the coast when the Apaches caught and killed them all. Apaches put the gold in the cave."

"If the Apaches killed them all, how do you know about it?" asked one of the Kansans.

"All but one," the prospector amended. "All but one. He drew a map so he could come back and get the gold, but he never made it. Never came back."

"Where is the cave?"

The old man gulped down his drink, slammed the glass to the bar and said, "Easy to find once you know where to look. That's the key. Knowing where to look. There're clues. Burned wagons. Remains of burned wagons still there after all these years, but they're hard to see now. Not much more than charred wood and burned wheels. Bones around them, too. On the bank of a shallow river."

"Gold there?"

Grinning, the prospector pointed to his glass. When it was filled again, he said, "Nope. That's just a clue. Apaches took it to a cave. Stacked it inside and then left it. A sacred place for them now."

"Crap," said one of the Kansans.

"Found it myself," said the prospector. "Looked for it more'n thirty years. Looked for it since I was a young man. Found it, too."

"You got a map?" one man asked again.

The old man hesitated and then chuckled. "Got a map right here." He pointed an index finger at his temple. "Only map I need is right here."

"Come on, Jake. The guy's crazy."

The prospector finished his drink and waited, but no one spoke again. The two men from Kansas emptied their glasses and then waved off the bartender. "Wasted too much money," said Jake. "Too many wild tales." They walked out together.

"How about you?" said the old man, looking back at Travis. "Buy me a drink?"

Travis shook his head.

The prospector carried his glass over and set it on the table. "Name's Crockett. Caleb Crockett."

"David Travis."

"Well, Mister Travis, I noticed that you don't say much."

"Don't say anything unless I've got something to say."

Crockett pulled out the chair and dropped into it. "I told the truth."

"Sure. I've heard those stories since I was a kid. Caves full of Spanish gold. Only a fool'd believe them."

"I saw it myself. Stood in the cave and looked right at it. Saw the burned wagons and the bones of the dead."

"Sand'd cover them after all this time."

"Covered most of it," said Crockett, nodding. "Covered most of it but didn't cover it all and I saw it."

"Saw it yourself?"

"I know where it is. Found it and saw it. After more'n thirty years."

"Then why don't you have any gold?"

"Gold's heavy. Too heavy to carry on the back. Need a wagon and a team of horses. Then I'll have all the money I need."

Travis finished his drink and glanced up at the bartender who stood leaning against the wall, arms folded across his chest. He was no longer listening.

"You want to help me. Buy the horses and we'll share the gold. There's more'n enough for both of us. More'n enough to last us both for the rest of our lives."

"Buy the horses and the food and everything else we'd need," said Travis. "And the whiskey, too."

"Just a bottle," said Crockett. "Just one bottle."

Travis pushed back his chair. The legs scraped the wooden floor. He stood. "I'm not interested."

"Gold," said Crockett. "We don't even have to dig it up. It's there for the taking. Waiting for us."

"No thanks," said Travis. He dropped a dollar on the table, knowing that the old prospector would pick it up. That was why he'd done it. Give the old man money for something to eat without really handing him charity. With that, he headed for the door. As he stepped out into the bright sunlight, he heard Crockett say to the bartender, "Bring me another drink and I'll tell you all about the gold."

Chapter Four
Sweetwater, Texas
August 7, 1863

The room hadn't been worth the price. The mattress had been little more than a sack stuffed with straw, the walls had been so thin that every noise from the hallway and every word spoken on the street had drifted up to him. The air inside had been heavy with humidity and had failed to circulate, making it difficult to sleep. Just lying on the bed and staring up at the ceiling had been enough to work up a sweat even after Travis had removed most of his clothes.

The hot desert air blew in the open window. There was a dull, flickering light from outside, and the noise boiling up from the saloon kept him awake. Men were shouting at one another. Arguments about the war in the East, or the desert in the West, or the Indians everywhere. Travis rolled to his side, glanced at the window, and then closed his eyes. He tried to ignore the sounds and the heat.

Later, light pouring through the window woke him. He sat up and looked out. The heat hadn't broken during the night and neither had the humidity. He rubbed a hand over his face and then wiped the sweat on the soaked mattress cover. Standing, he walked to the window and looked out and down.

A single horse was hitched to the rail in front of the saloon. The place was still open, the arguments still going but quieter now, and Travis wondered if the bartender ever slept.

He turned away from the window and walked to the water basin set on the top of a chest. He poured water from a pitcher in it, splashed the tepid liquid on his face, and then dried himself on the small cotton towel.

There was no reason to shave, especially since he didn't have a sharp razor. He'd wait until he could find a barber. He dressed and then looked at the pistol in its black leather holster.

Downstairs he was directed into the restaurant. It looked to be an afterthought. Those who had built the hotel realized that the travelers were going to need food, so they had cobbled the restaurant to the side of the building. The floor was bare wooden planks, the walls had been painted once, but the color had faded. A single door led out into the street, and it stood open. One of the two windows on either side of it was broken and had been repaired with greased paper.

There were three tables, each surrounded by four chairs but no linen. There were lamps on each of the walls with soot marks above them on the ceiling.

Travis entered and took the table closest to the window so that he could watch the street. He wasn't looking for anyone or anything in particular, but then, he never knew what he might see out there. It was a way of avoiding unpleasant surprises.

A girl, no more than twenty, appeared. Her brown hair was pinned up, although a few strands had escaped. She wore a stained apron and there was a smear of flour along her jaw line. Sweat was beaded on her upper lip. She looked as if she had already put in a full day.

"Breakfast?" she asked.

"With..?"

"You get what we got. A steak, some eggs, and a few potatoes. We got coffee and we got some milk if it ain't spoiled yet."

"Whatever," said Travis.

While he waited, he watched the street. A skinny dog walked along it and then darted around a building, disappearing down the alley. One man then staggered out of the saloon, held a hand up to shade his eyes as if surprised by the brightness of the sun, and walked away.

The waitress returned, set a plate in front of him, put a knife and fork down next to the plate, and asked, "You want the coffee?"

"Sure."

She left and came back with a mug and a huge coffee pot clutched in her hand. The wooden handle looked well used. She filled the cup, glanced at him, and then whirled, heading back to the kitchen.

Travis turned his attention to his breakfast. He salted the steak and then cut into it.. He took a bite and then tried the eggs. They were runny and the potatoes were cold. Travis found that he didn't care about that because he knew there were men still at war who were chewing on maggot-infested hardtack and eating biscuits that were as hard as rocks. They were the men who had stayed on the field after Gettysburg, the men who had stayed in the army after the slaughter that battle had been. There was nothing as bad as that here. Nothing for him to complain about here. He put the image out of his mind.

He ate slowly, sipping coffee and keeping an eye on the street. He put down his fork as the old prospector appeared in the doorway of the saloon. He paused long enough to put his hat on his head, tug at the waist of his pants, and then step off, walking along the front of the building.

From the unsteady gait, Travis knew that the prospector had spent the night spinning stories about the Spanish gold. It looked as if more than one man had volunteered drinks to keep the old prospector talking.

Travis finished the last of his coffee as the prospector disappeared into the early morning shadows. Travis stood and dug in his pocket for a dollar. He dropped it on the table but before he could turn, he saw the two Kansans move from the shadows in the alley near the saloon.

"Now what the hell?" he said.

The men stopped at the door of the saloon, peered in and then began walking again, looking as if they were following the old man.

"You want anything else?"

Travis turned, surprised by the woman. He hadn't heard her approach. He looked at her. "No. Thank you."

She picked up the empty plate, dropped the fork onto the center of it, put the mug there, and left. She didn't say another word to him.

Now Travis looked back to the street, but it was vacant again. The men from Kansas were nowhere to be seen. He leaned forward and saw only a man on horseback.

Travis walked into the lobby and started for the stairs, but then stopped. Instead he turned and walked out the open front door. He stood for a moment in the early morning light and was aware that the stable was close. He stepped down into the street.

To his right was a wagon parked near the front of the feed store. A woman sat on the bench loosely holding the reins. Two men stood in the doorway talking.

To the left was the edge of the town. A small house surrounded by a short adobe fence. And opposite him was a series of buildings including the office of the territory newspaper. There was an alley, and along the side wall a set of steps led up into a second floor room.

There was something in the air. Travis was sure. The appearance of those two Kansans right after the old prospector meant something. They were following him. Waiting for him. Travis couldn't convince himself that anyone would be dumb enough to believe an old story of gold hidden by the Spanish told by a man hustling drinks.

Just as Travis had decided that nothing was wrong, there was a single scream cut off suddenly. That had to come from the alley on the other side of the saloon. Travis stepped down into the street and started across.

There was a second shout, "NO!" and then silence. Travis broke into a run. He leaped up on the walk and slipped closer to the side of the building. He moved along it and then peeked around into the alley.

The old prospector lay on the ground, his hands up to protect his face. One of the Kansans bent over him, his fist raised as if he was about to strike. The other stood watching. Both of them wore guns though neither had drawn a weapon.

"The map, old man," said the one with his fist raised. "Where's the map?"

"No map," said the prospector. "No map. I memorized it. No map. I told you. No map."

"Leave him," said the other man. "He's full of it. Just trying to scam drinks."

"No," said the prospector suddenly. "The gold is real."

"Well, hell, old man," said the Kansan. "I was just trying to help you."

The first man knelt, his right knee on the soft, wet ground. He struck the prospector and the old man moaned.

Without thinking, Travis stepped around the corner of the building. "Leave him be."

The standing man turned, reaching for the pistol on his hip. He grinned when he saw that Travis was unarmed.

"Shouldn't give orders if you can't back them up."

Travis didn't move. He watched both the Kansans. "The old man is crazy. Let him go."

The man who had been holding the prospector up, dropped him and then whipped out his knife. He put it to the prospector's throat. "Go or I kill him."

Travis took a step forward and then froze as both men moved to face him. "There's no gold," said Travis.

There was a moment's hesitation and then the man with the knife struck. He plunged the blade into the prospector's chest. He straightened, the blade of the knife dripping blood. The Kansan grinned. "Now he lies to no one else."

With that, both men turned and ran down the alley. They stopped at the far corner of the building. One of them turned, looked at Travis, and then both of them were gone.

Travis ran to the old prospector, trying to remember his name. He'd mentioned it the day before, but Travis was terrible with names.

Kneeling next to the old man, he said, "Take it easy old-timer. Take it easy." He pulled at the blood-soaked cloth so that he could examine the wound. It didn't look bad. There was a lot of blood, staining the faded flannel shirt and dripping to the ground, but Travis had seen men hurt worse than that survive. Hell, he'd seen men hurt worse than that stay in the fight until the battle was over.

The old man reached up and grasped Travis's arm. "Thanks," he gasped. "Thanks."

"Got to get you to the doc," said Travis. He started to lift, to help the man to his feet but the prospector groaned.

"No. Too late. Too late."

"Don't be foolish."

The man moaned quietly and closed his eyes. His breathing became ragged. He clutched at the dirt, his knuckles turning white. He opened his eyes and looked up into the bright blue of the morning sky.

"You've got to tell her," he said.

"Tell who?" asked Travis.

He grinned. His teeth were blood-smeared. Travis had seen that a few times in the war. It was always a bad sign. It meant bleeding in the lungs or the stomach and that the wounded man would live only a short time more. Maybe a couple of minutes or maybe a couple of hours.

"They didn't get it," he said. "I hid it. I know people. They think they can steal it and they will, so I always hide it. But now you got to take it to her."

"Who?" asked Travis.

"My daughter. It belongs to her now." He turned and stared up at Travis, but the eyes were blank, like those of a stuffed animal in a museum. No life in them.

"The doctor," said Travis.

"No time. Too late for me. You take it to my daughter and tell her to give you half. Reward."

"Let's get you to the doctor and then we'll talk about rewards."

The prospector coughed, spraying blood. His skin was waxy, looking unnatural, unreal.

"My daughter," he said. "Stable." And then his eyes glazed over.

Travis stared down at him and knew that he was dead. He'd seen enough men die to know when it happened.

He laid the man's head back into the dirt and then tried to close the eyes. He stood up and turned. There were two men and a woman standing at the end of the alley looking at him.

"What happened?" asked one of the men.

"Get the marshal," said Travis. "This man has been murdered."

Chapter Five
Sweetwater, Texas
August 7, 1863

Travis stood looking out the marshal's window, watching as the streets filled with people. There were those standing outside the saloon, waiting to enter, and those who were at the feed store and those at the general store. There was a kid chasing a dog and a man with a rake trying to clean the street, sweeping the manure up under the boardwalks and out of the way.

"You don't know who the men were?" asked the marshal.

Travis turned. "They were in the saloon yesterday. First time I ever saw them."

"I doubt they'll be back," he said.

Travis nodded. He moved toward the desk. A small desk pushed back against the wall. There was a cabinet over it holding a rack of rifles, a chain through their triggerguards. A pot bellied stove stood in the corner with a coffee pot on it, but it didn't look as if either had been used in a long time.

"Man said that he had a daughter, but I don't know her name or where to find her. He asked me to take his belongings to her."

"You inclined to do it?"

Travis shrugged. "I've nothing better to do except that I don't know who she is."

"Man's name," said the marshal, "was Crockett . . ."

"That's right," said Travis, remembering. "Caleb Crockett."

The marshal bent and lifted a well-worn saddlebag to the top of his desk. "This is all the old man had except for his mule over in the stable. I guess it all belongs to the daughter now."

Travis nodded at it. "Any clue about where she might be?"

"Hammetsville. A little town about fifty miles from here. Not much more than a stage stop." The marshal pushed a leatherbound book from the saddlebag. "Name's in here."

Travis rubbed a hand over his face. He glanced at the saddlebags and then thought of the old man in the street, dying because he had told a story of Spanish gold. He touched the soft leather. "I'll take it to her."

"Not much here. An old shirt, a knife, and some papers. And the book." The marshal looked up at Travis. "A lifetime of work and it can be stuffed into one small bag."

"There is the daughter," said Travis.

"There is that," replied the marshal. He pushed the saddlebag across the desk. "When do you think you'll be leaving? Today?"

"There some hurry?"

The marshal narrowed his eyes. "We haven't had much trouble around here lately."

Travis understood, though he didn't like it. He'd only found the results. He hadn't starting anything, but then the marshal was just protecting his job. Get everyone out of town except those who belong and things would continue to run smoothly.

"As soon as I get my gear at the hotel, I'll be gone."

The marshal grinned, nodded, and stood. He held out a hand. "We're delighted that you visited our town. Please come back soon." He did not sound sincere.

Jake Freeman stood on a ridge just outside of town. The sun was hot on his back and he held one hand up to shade his eyes from the brightness of the desert around him. Behind him Matthew Crosby sat on one horse and held the reins of the second. He had pulled his hat down low and had closed his eyes against the brightness.

"Can't see the son of a bitch," said Freeman. "Went into the marshal's office and hasn't come out."

"The old man has a daughter," said Crosby.

Freeman dropped his hand and turned so that he was looking up at

Crosby. "That piece of information does us no good because we don't know where she is."

"If you hadn't been quite so fast with the knife, we might have found that out."

"That old man wasn't going to talk to us, and I didn't want him talking to anyone else."

"Well he did."

Freeman nodded and said, "But he won't talk anymore. Now we'll just wait here and see what we can see."

He turned back to watch the main street. He saw someone exit the marshal's office carrying a bag. The man walked to the hotel and disappeared inside.

"Looks like our boy has found himself something," said Freeman.

"We going to visit him?" Crosby pushed his hat back so that he could look down into the street.

"If we wait, he might come to visit us and that way no one will be able to see or hear anything."

Travis buckled on his gunbelt and then turned slowly, taking a last look around the room. Satisfied that he had picked up everything that belonged to him, he grabbed the saddlebag and left. Outside, he walked across the street to the livery stable. He entered there and moved toward the rear where his horse waited.

A man came out of the shadows. "Help you?"

"Thought I'd pick up my horse."

"Leaving us?"

"Yes."

"While you saddle up, I'll figure the bill."

"I'll be taking that mule, too," he said, pointing into a stall.

"Can't do that. Belongs to someone."

"He's dead," said Travis. "I'm taking it to the relatives."

When the man hesitated, Travis added, "You can check with the marshal."

"No. I suppose it's okay, if the marshal approved it." He cocked his head to the side. "Who pays the bill?"

Travis shrugged and then said, "I'll do it."

"Be with you in a moment." The man turned and vanished into the shadows again.

Travis opened the stall and entered, moving along the side of it, watching where he put his feet. He put a hand on the horse's flank and rubbed it, letting the beast know that he was there. When he reached the front of the stall, he patted the horse's nose, and then gently pushed so that the horse would back up and out.

When he got the horse saddled, the livery man reappeared. "I make it six bits."

"You're sure?"

"Six bits."

Travis paid the man and then waited as he got the mule ready to move. The man gave him the leader, and Travis walked his horse and the mule out into the sunlight. He put a hand up to shade his eyes and scanned the street and the ground beyond it. That had been something he learned in the army. Survey the terrain, when possible, before riding up into it. That could save some nasty surprises.

Travis swung up into the saddle. He sat for a moment, wondering why he was about to ride fifty miles to tell a woman he didn't know that her father, whom he hadn't known either, had died. He owed her or her father nothing. Except that a dying man had asked him to do it. Travis had said he would and now felt obligated to do it.

He rode out of town and followed the road up to the top of a ridge. He stopped briefly and looked back down at the town. Not much more than a flyspeck on the map. A few houses, a few buildings, and nothing around it except open desert. Hot winds and dust devils swirled.

He turned again and rode on into the next valley. It stretched out into the distance, a glowing gray hell with no sign of water or green vegetation. Far away was the hint of mountains. They were vague shapes shimmering in the heat.

Travis let the horse have its head. It followed the road along the floor of the valley. It didn't bother with the dried clumps of sagebrush and ignored the sharp spines of the prickly pear. It had been well fed at the stable. Well fed and well watered.

He had come to a sharp bend in the road, next to a dry riverbed. There was a stand of stunted trees growing in the corner, their leaves rattling in the light breeze, and across the riverbed was a rocky ledge sloping upward.

There was no warning. Travis saw nothing and heard nothing. There was a sudden splash in the dust of the road and an instant later, the report of a rifle. Without a thought, Travis rolled to his right, off his horse and to the ground. As he landed, the horse leaped forward, ran a few steps and then stopped, confused. The mule turned, bucked, and headed back up the road.

Travis continued to roll, his eyes on the rocks across the riverbed. He scrambled into a slight depression and drew his revolver, knowing that it would do him no good. Not if his attacker was in the rocks with a rifle. The range was too great for it.

For ten minutes he lay there, his eyes moving slowly up the slope, searching for the rifleman. He felt sweat trickle down his back and his side. He wiped his forehead on the sleeve of his shirt and continued to search.

Finally he knew that he would have to move. If the gunman was still there, Travis could wait all day. He was probably in the shade with a canteen. Travis, on the other hand, was in the blazing sun with no water. In an hour it would be unbearable in the depression. In two, he would not be able to think rationally as the sun baked him. The only thing he could do was make a run for it and hope that the first shot indicated how bad a marksman the man in the rocks was.

Taking a deep breath, Travis pushed himself to his feet and then sprinted toward his horse.

Chapter Six
Outside Sweetwater, Texas
August 7, 1863

"You missed him. How could you miss?

Crosby shrugged and cocked his weapon, but it was too late then. The man had rolled off his horse and was out of sight. The horse had run fifty or sixty feet before stopping.

"I could shoot his horse."

"No," said Freeman. "He'd just go back to Sweetwater and that's not going to do us any good."

"So what are we going to do?"

Freeman didn't answer right away. He stared down across the dry river-bed. The man was out of sight, hidden behind the scrub or rocks. He wasn't moving around, so that it was impossible to spot him. He knew what he was doing.

"Seems to me," said Freeman, "that we should just follow him. Stay back, out of sight, and see where he's going. We can take him anytime we want to."

"He knows that we're out here," said Crosby.

"No. He knows that a shot was fired, but that's all he knows. One shot. Hell, it might not even have been fired at him. Stray round. Strange things happen on the desert."

Crosby slipped back deeper into the shadows. He pulled his hat off and wiped his forehead. He glanced at the rifle and then at Freeman. "Maybe he doesn't know a thing."

"He's got that old man's mule. He wouldn't have it if he didn't know something. We'll just bide our time." Freeman turned around and watched the scene below him.

Travis reached his horse easily. He grabbed the reins and then knelt behind it, looking up into the rocks. He held his pistol in his right hand, the hammer back for a quick shot, but there was no movement anywhere. Nothing to betray the ambushers. High overhead a single bird wheeled and that was the only thing he could see moving.

Travis stood, the horse between him and the rifleman, holstered his pistol and swung himself up into the saddle. He leaned forward, grabbing the horse's neck and slipped to the right, supporting his weight with the stirrup. That made it difficult for anyone on the other side of the riverbed to see him. He dug his heels into the horse and it leaped forward. He pulled back on the reins, slowed, and then turned. Still no movement in the rocks. Hunching forward, he raced back to where the prospector's mule stood, nibbling at a dried-up bush.

Leaning forward, he snagged the roped tied to the bridle. He took a final, quick look at the rocks, and then whirling around, dug his heels in. With the mule in tow, he rode along the bank of the river, still trying to spot the ambushers and to get out of there. He ran past the bend in the dry river and the copse of trees, and then up, toward the top of the ridgeline.

When he reached it, he stopped and jumped from the saddle. He left his pistol in the holster as he knelt, scanning the rocks around the riverbed but still saw nothing down there. No signs of anyone or any horse.

Shaking his head, he lead his horse and the mule from the top of the ridgeline before he climbed back into the saddle. One shot was a lousy ambush. Maybe they, whoever they were, had not been shooting at him. Maybe it was a stray round. Maybe it was just a big coincidence.

"I don't know," he told his horse. "I just don't know."

The bartender had rarely had so much business. The men were crowded three deep in front of him, and he had been able to raise his prices with no one complaining. He rushed from one end of the bar to the other, slopping his watered-down booze into glasses that he didn't bother to wash because no one cared about that either.

A thick haze of blue smoke hung in the air that the breeze from outside failed to dissipate. A few men were smoking cigars. Most had cigarettes.

"Tell us again," yelled one of the men.

"Tell you what?" shouted the bartender. "I told you it all four times. The old prospector was crazy. Talking of bars of gold hidden in a cave."

"I've heard that before," said a man at the bar. He held his drink up and turned so that he could face the crowd. "Heard that story for years."

"It's a crock."

"No. No. Where there's smoke, there's a fire. And the Apaches do have ceremonial caves."

"Bull."

The man turned and looked at his accuser. "You ever been out there. Out to the west. Into the territories?"

"No."

"Then shut up." The man drained his drink.

"What do you know?" asked someone else.

The man put his glass on the bar and waited. The bartender, knowing a good thing when he saw it, filled the glass so that the man would spin his tale. Even if the man didn't pay cash for the booze, the others would. He was earning the drink by telling the story of Spanish gold.

"Apaches," said the man, retrieving his glass and sipping from it, "Apaches don't understand the value of gold. They see it as a gift from their gods, something they are to protect. If they leave it alone and protect it, they will be strong. If they let others see it and steal it, then they lose their power."

"Bull," said the accuser again.

"No bull. Fact. There is a valley that no one has seen since the time of the Spanish. A valley filled with gold. Nuggets as big as eggs laying on the ground. A river so thick in the dust that you can't stick a pan in it without showing color. And veins of it as tall as a man."

"Where's this valley?"

The man laughed. "Only the Apache know and they guard it with their lives. To share that secret is to die."

"Then how do you?"

"I know and that's all that matters." He took a drink. "No white man has ever seen that valley. Except once. The Spanish found the valley and that's where the gold came from."

One man pounded his empty glass on the bar waiting for a refill. He didn't take his eyes off the man who was doing all the talking.

"They stayed there for weeks using savages brought up from Mexico to do the hard work. To do the mining. They smelted it right there, cutting down the few trees that grew along the river. Smelted it all and made it into bars that were almost too heavy to lift."

"How do you know?"

The man smiled knowingly and finished his drink. "I just know."

"Where is this valley?"

"You'd never get there. Apaches watch it all the time now. After the Spanish violated it, they watch and kill anyone who is getting too close to it. Valley's not important anyway. In the valley you'd have to mine the gold and smelt it and carry it out, all with the Apaches around to stop you. Valley's not important."

"So what is?"

"The cave. Spanish got some of the gold out of the valley and were taking it back to Spain when the Apaches caught them. The Apaches reclaimed the treasure and then hid it."

"Bull," said the accuser again. "A lot of bull."

The bartender, sensing that the drinkers were going to start drifting away, raised his voice. "Not bull. I stood right here yesterday and listened to a prospector who had seen that gold. Seen it with his own eyes."

"What'd he see?"

The bartender put down the bottle he held and moved to the center of the bar. He waited until all the eyes were on him and then told the old prospector's story again, slowly, watching as the men finished their drinks. Before he ended the story, he moved among them, pouring more booze into their glasses and collecting more of their money.

Satisfied for the moment, he said to them, "Old man said that it wasn't far from here. Hidden in a cave where the Apaches took it. More gold than one man could spend in a lifetime. More gold than anyone could ever need."

"Then we should go get it," shouted a man. "If it's that easy, we should go get it."

"What about the Apaches?"

"There's enough of us, and the Apaches aren't going to be a problem."

The bartender grinned to himself and began pouring booze again. The only gold to be found was in the pockets of the men in the saloon and he was finding quite a bit of it.

Chapter Seven
Hammetsville, Texas
August 22, 1863

The Crockett house, a small, adobe structure with a tile roof, was on the outskirts of Hammetsville. There was a single door, windows on either side, and a chimney on one side for heat in the winter or to cook in the summer. Nights and winters in the desert could get very cold.

A Joshua tree was growing in front of the house, and an adobe wall surrounded part of the yard. Travis saw smoke coming from the chimney and knew that someone was home. He stopped near the gate and slipped from the saddle. He wrapped the rein around the post but didn't tie it. No reason for that. The lead for the mule was tied to his saddle horn.

He stood in the gate for a moment, looking at the house. During the ride from Sweetwater he had thought about what he was going to say. Nothing seemed to be adequate. If he had known Crockett better, or if he knew the daughter, the words might have been easy to find. But he didn't know if the daughter liked her father, if she believed in him, or if there had been a family rift that meant she didn't care or that she wouldn't care.

As he walked toward the door, it opened and a woman appeared. Travis, for some reason, had thought of the daughter as a little girl. But the person in the door wasn't a little girl. She was a woman who might have been twenty or twenty-five. Her long hair was hanging loose to her waist. She was about five five and had dark brown eyes.

He stopped short and took off his hat. "Miss Crockett?"

She wiped her hands on the apron she wore and nodded. "I'm Emma Crockett."

"Yes ma'am," he said. He glanced up at the sky and saw that it was about noon, maybe a little after. The heat of the day was building. There was a bird somewhere calling, but Travis couldn't see it. He knew that he was delaying, as long as possible, telling her the bad news.

"Would you care for something to drink?" she asked, wiping her face with her apron. "Going to be real hot."

"No ma'am." He stood looking up at her framed in the doorway. She was a pretty woman with a narrow face and delicate features. As she wiped the back of her hand over her lips he wished that he hadn't brought the news. He didn't want to hurt her and was suddenly afraid that she would blame him for her father's death.

"I've some bad news," he said finally, quietly.

"I know," she said, looking past him. "He's not coming home this time."

"I'm afraid not ma'am. How did you know?"

She didn't answer. She turned and walked back into the house. She left the door open but said nothing to him.

Travis stood out there for a moment wondering what to do, and then moved to the door. He looked in. She was sitting in a rocker that faced the fireplace. There was a table to one side, two chairs near it, and then a huge bed opposite the fireplace. A cedar trunk sat at the foot of it. He wondered if the bed was hers.

"Miss Crockett?" he said.

She didn't look at him. "I knew he wouldn't be coming home this time. I knew. And then I saw you with his mule. He'd never have given it up if he was still alive. That's all I had to see to know."

"I'm sorry." He turned and pointed back toward the mule. "I have his things here. I brought them . . ."

She stood suddenly, blinking rapidly. "Yes," she said, her voice tight. "I'm being rude. Please come in. Can I get you something? I was just going to make my lunch and you're welcome to join me."

She was beginning to talk faster and faster. She was keeping her mouth going so that she wouldn't think about what he had just told her. Anything to fill her mind so that she wouldn't have to think. He'd seen the same thing on battlefields when the fighting had ended.

Travis didn't know what to do. He wanted to give her the mule and her father's possessions and leave. And he wanted to stay to comfort her and to help her. He turned away from her and said, "There are some things that I could bring in for you. Your father's things."

"Please," she said.

Travis didn't wait for more. He walked out the door and to the mule. He untied the pack and dropped it to the ground. For a moment he sifted through it to make sure there was nothing in it that she shouldn't see. He crouched there, thinking about all the men who had died at Gettysburg and all the other men who had to ride out to inform the families. Thousands had been told that fathers or brothers or husbands would not be coming home. The difference was that Travis hadn't been among those who had to do it until now.

He glanced up at the door of the house. It was still open, waiting for him to return. He stood, brushed the dust from his knees, and picked up the saddlebags.

Inside he found her hunched over the sink, a hand to her face and her shoulders shaking. On the cutting board near her were vegetables and a knife.

"Where should I put these things?" he asked quietly, not sure of what to do.

She pointed at the table. A moment later she sniffed and said, "I'm sorry. This is really no surprise. He was getting old and he was pushing too hard."

Travis stood quietly for a moment, and when he could think of nothing else, said, "I'll be going now."

"No," she said. "You must stay. You'll have lunch before you go."

"No ma'am, I couldn't impose. Not now."

"You went out of your way to bring those things to me. The least I can do is feed you."

Travis was about to refuse again but then realized she wanted the company. If he left, there would be no one around for her to talk to.

"Is there any family around?" he asked.

"No. I'm being terrible." She gestured toward the table. "Sit down and I'll find something for you to eat."

"If you're sure that it won't be too much trouble."

"I'm glad to have something to do."

Freeman lay on the top of the hill looking down into the valley. He could easily see Travis's horse and the old man's mule outside the cabin. He watched as Travis came out once, got the saddlebags and took them back inside.

"That's it," said Freeman.

Crosby was sitting with his back to a rock, his hat pulled low. "We take him now?"

"He's doing our work for us," said Freeman. "Why interrupt him?"

"I don't like this. I want to know where we're heading. We don't know that, and he could give us the slip. We could find ourselves wandering around lost in the desert."

"I kept us close to him until he got here, didn't I?"

"But that woman. She'll know where the gold is. We could make her tell us," said Crosby. "Then we wouldn't have to worry about either of them."

"No reason for that. No reason to make this harder than it has to be. We sit back and watch, and when the time comes, we can move in and take the gold."

Crosby pushed his hat back and said, "I've been thinking about that. Why do we want it all? We could just sit back, as you say, let them take what they can and then get the rest. The old man said there was more than enough for that."

"Because there is no reason to share it," said Freeman. "They find it for us and then we take it. All of it. If you don't like that, then head on out. I won't need any help."

"What's going on down there now?" asked Crosby to change the subject.

Freeman turned his attention back to the cabin. "He's inside again."

Crosby crawled forward and stretched out next to Freeman. "Think he's going to stay?"

"Hell, he's just after the gold like the rest of us. That old man must have said something to him before he died. Now he's pumping the woman to see what she knows. We stick close to him and we're going to get to the gold. That's all we've got to do.

The Sweetwater bartender had closed his saloon shortly after the old prospector had been killed. William Davis had decided that there was enough to the story that he was going in search of the gold. Now he, along with twelve others, were heading toward El Paso. That was the one thing the prospector had said while he had been in the saloon when there was no one else present. To find the gold, you had to ride north from El Paso.

They had collected prospectors slowly. A half-dozen men in Sweetwater who had nothing better to do, including Jason Culhaine, George Bailey, Virgil Webster, Peter Ramsey, Paul Haught and Stephen Vogol. Another man, Jonathan Whitney, who worked on a ranch where the cattle had died because there had been no rain and there was no reason to stay, had joined them along the trail. Two men, Daniel Bourne and Albert Martin, who had been working a mine that had produced huge piles of clay and sand but no gold, had also joined. Davis thought they had just decided to start digging with no clue about what they were doing. They had believed the gold was in the ground, and all you had to do was dig for it.

They had come across a man, Thomas Kincaid, sitting on the side of the road, looking at his sweat-covered horse. He had been chased by Indians, he claimed. He and his partner had been attacked for no reason. He'd gotten away but the Indians had caught his friend, dragging him screaming from his horse.

"Indians aren't real hostile anymore," said Davis. "No reason for them to attack you unless you started it."

Kincaid had looked at Davis but had not replied. He joined them, not because they were going for the gold, but because there were so many of them riding toward El Paso. The gold was secondary.

Now they were sitting around a campfire while two men worked at cooking something to eat. A jackrabbit that Whitney had shot, some beans they had bought in the store in Sweetwater, and coffee boiled in a blackened pot.

"How long ago you run into those Indians?" asked Jason Culhaine. He had been working in the general store for free food, a place to sleep, and a buck a week spending money.

"Watched them for a couple of days," said Thomas Kincaid. "Saw them in the distance, saw their fire at night, but didn't think much of it."

"Yeah," said Davis. "If they let you see them, then they weren't worried about you. You see the army?

"Which one?"

"Hell, either one. Rebels been working with some of the tribes, and the Federals have been trying to protect the settlers in the territories. Some militia around charged with that job."

"Didn't see any soldiers," said Kincaid. "Didn't see anybody but the Indians."

George Bailey was crouched near the fire holding onto the wooden handle of a huge pot. He was stirring the beans in it, letting them heat slowly. Bailey had done odd jobs for whoever needed things done. He had been only too happy to get out of Sweetwater.

"Food's about done," he said.

Davis got up and walked over to where the horses were tethered. He reached into his saddlebag and brought out a bottle. One of the few that he had taken from the saloon before he closed the doors, locking them.

He returned to the fire and sat down again. "Tomorrow we should reach El Paso. In celebration, I brought this."

Kincaid held out his cup. "I could use that."

Bailey glanced over his shoulder. "You never told us why the Indians attacked you."

"I don't know. We were breaking camp when they appeared on the ridge looking down on us. Maybe then, twelve of them, sitting there, just watching us. I didn't like it. Neither did Isaac. We decided it was time to get out. We mounted and began to ride off. Slowly. They started down after us and a moment later the chase was on."

"So you left him," said Bailey.

"His horse went down. I stopped and turned, but they were on him. Nothing I could do for him except get killed myself. I got out."

"Noble," said Davis.

"What the hell would you have done?" asked Kincaid, his voice rising in anger.

"Shot him," said Davis quietly, staring into Kincaid's dark eyes. "Shot him myself so them savages wouldn't have him to torture."

"Sure," said Kincaid. "Sure."

Bailey lifted the pot out of the fire and set it on the ground to his left. Steam rolled off the top of it as the beans bubbled. He looked at Davis. "What do we do once we get to El Paso?"

"We lay in the supplies we need, plus the pack animals for a couple of weeks in the desert. Once we find the gold, we dump the excess food, load the animals and make our way to the nearest town."

"You know where the gold is?" asked Kincaid.

Davis turned to face the other man. "I have a good idea about that. It's one that I don't care to share with anyone right now."

"Hell," said Bailey, "that old coot said there was more than enough for all of us. Too much for us to carry away. Enough to make us all rich."

"Right," said Davis. "I just want to make sure I have my chance to carry some of it away. Once we find it, it's every man for himself."

"What about the Apaches?" asked Bailey. He nodded toward Kincaid. "Sounds like they're around and sounds like they're hostile."

"We'll avoid them," said Davis. He looked into the faces of the men sitting around the fire and then picked up a tin plate, scooped beans out of a pot, and asked, "When's the rabbit going to be ready?"

"Couple of minutes."

"Good," said Davis. "I'm real hungry."

Chapter Eight
Hammetsville, Texas
August 22, 1863

"I don't understand," Emma Crockett said. "If you don't believe the story, why did you bother to search for me?"

Travis, sitting at the table, the remains of the meal in front of him, said, "Your father asked me to tell you what happened to him. I thought it was only right that someone brought you the information."

"You think he was a crazy old man," she said. She held up a hand to stop the protest. "No, I can see it in your face. You think he's crazy. Think he was crazy." Her voice caught as she said that. "That anyone who believes in stories of Spanish gold is crazy."

"It's not that," said Travis.

She dropped into the chair opposite him. Once again Travis realized how pretty she was. Light olive skin, long black hair, and dark, penetrating eyes. He wondered why there wasn't a husband and then wondered if there had been but he was off fighting in the war.

"My father was not crazy," she said. "I can prove it to you if I want."

"Maybe I should be going," said Travis, not wanting to leave.

"Did you ever see the map?" she asked.

"He said that he had it in his head."

Now she smiled. "He did. But there was a map drawn long ago. A real map. Would you like to see it?"

"That'll tell me where the gold is," said Travis, grinning. "I could get it all for myself."

"No, there is too much for that. Besides, in two hundred years the landmarks have changed. The riverbed has shifted slightly, trees have died and new ones have grown, and the names of places have changed."

"Then what good is the map?" asked Travis.

"It puts you into the right place and makes it that much easier to find the gold. You wait right here."

She got up and crossed the room and knelt in front of the cedar chest where she had put the saddlebags. She dug through them until she came up with an old book. Standing, she waved it at him. "This will prove that my father wasn't crazy."

"I never said he was."

She set the book in front of him. Travis opened it and found that it was a handwritten document. A diary. "Where'd you get this?"

"It was in my mother's family. When she died, the only thing she left was that trunk and a few things in it. Among them was the diary."

Travis scanned it but couldn't read it. "It's all in Spanish."

"Of course. Alverez, the man who wrote it, was Spanish. Had come to the New World from Spain."

Travis flipped through it, able to decipher only the faded writing of the dates. It was started in March, 1692 and was kept until August, 1694.

Travis pushed it toward her. "Can you read it?"

"Of course." She took the diary, turned, and flipped through it. Slowly, she read the passages that dealt with the Spanish convoy that was taking the gold from the mountains in the north, toward the coast in the southeast. She read of the attack and Alverez's escape. And she read of the Apaches moving the gold from the wagons to a cave.

While she read, Travis studied the shape of her face and the line of her jaw. She had perfect teeth. As she turned the pages, he noticed that her fingers were long and slender. He was glad that he had gone out of his way to find her.

When she finished reading, she looked up at him. "See? We're not crazy." She returned his stare.

"A diary doesn't prove a thing," said Travis. He reached out for his coffee cup but had finished it with his meal.

"In the back is the map." She opened to it. "See? You recognize it?"

Travis studied it. There were references to places he thought were now in New Mexico. Bottomless lakes far north of El Paso. He pointed to one point and said, "Part of the Guadalupe Mountains?"

"Lots of caves in that area," she said. "That was the real problem. Finding the right cave near a shallow river."

Travis looked up at her. "So that was what your father was doing. Poking into caves until he found the right one."

She closed the diary and stared at him. "There are clues outside it. The river and the burned wagons. The cave is in a cliff to the north of there."

Travis shook his head. "There's no gold no matter what that diary says. It's the dreams of a man who watched as his brother and his friends were killed."

"No," she said. "No. There is gold." She hesitated for a moment. "We could go get the gold. You and me."

Travis sat quietly. He looked first at the old diary and then up at the young woman. As he stared at her, he realized that the gold wasn't important. She was asking him to help find it. She trusted him enough to confide in him and show him the diary. There was nothing else that he had to do. No place that he had to go now that he had left the army after Gettysburg. They would be moving deeper into the territories and away from the war waging in the States. Away from the maneuvering armies who were searching for one another to eliminate one another. All he had to worry about were Indians, snakes, and scorpions. He was getting the better end of the deal.

"You don't know where to begin," said Travis.

Now she grinned broadly. "But I do. My father kept track of where had looked. No sense in covering the same ground twice. He hadn't seen the gold on his last trip. I know where he was going on this one. If he was telling others that he had seen the gold, it means he found it this time."

Travis studied the interior of the cabin. A dirt floor that had been swept a hundred times, a thousand, until it was as hard as brick. Windows without glass in them but with shutters to keep out the rain and the wind and even the snow. A large bed, big enough for two. It was a comfortable cabin. A place that Travis could learn to enjoy.

"Once we have the gold," she said, "you could go wherever you wanted. You could buy whatever you wanted."

"And you?" asked Travis.

"I want to return to Mexico. I want to show them that I'm more than a half-breed with no refinement. I'll show them that they were wrong about me and my mother."

"It's not going to be easy," said Travis.

"But it's something that we could do," she said, reaching out to touch his arm.

Travis felt a spark of excitement and tried to suppress it. He thought about what he was saying, and for the moment he could think of nothing he'd rather do.

While the others cleaned up from the noon meal, Davis sat astride his horse, watching. Kincaid's story of raiding Indians had him worried. Hostile Apaches could keep him from finding the gold. They could keep him from living to find the gold.

Bailey approached and looked up. "I think we're about ready now."

"El Paso tonight," he said. "We keep riding until we reach El Paso."

Bailey stood there thinking about the wife he'd left in Sweetwater. She was a good woman who didn't nag or fuss and who cooked his meals and treated his injuries. A solid woman who knew that he would run out on her someday. Now he was wondering if he shouldn't abandon the search and just ride on home. There were some things more important than gold.

"You sure you know where to find the treasure?" he asked again.

Davis leaned down, his elbow on his thigh. He lowered his voice. "I told you. That old man talked. I gave him whiskey and he gave me information. I know where to look. He told me exactly where to look."

Bailey glanced at the others. "You really want to share it with them?"

"George, from what that old man said, there is no reason to worry about it. There is enough gold there for all of us and another hundred if we cared to ask them. There's more than we could carry off in a year. There is no reason for us to be greedy."

"Not greedy," said Bailey, "cautious. One man can keep a secret. Two can if one of them is dead. You have a dozen men and there will be no secret."

"Except that I'm the only one who knows what the old man said while we were alone."

Bailey took off his hat and wiped the sweat from his face. "You said he had kin."

"Daughter who doesn't know anything. She's no danger to us. None at all."

"We don't know all these men. We could lose some of them in El Paso. They're not our friends. Not like Culhaine and the others from Sweetwater."

"I tell you, George, you're worrying about nothing. That old man told me that there was a wall of gold in that cave. Even if we wanted to try, we couldn't get it all. We couldn't carry it all off in a year."

Bailey saw that the others were ready to go. They were sitting on their horses, staring into the bright morning sunshine.

To Davis he said, "If you're sure about that."

"I'm positive. Besides, the extra guns might come in handy if we run into that raiding party."

"I'll trust you on this one," said Bailey.

"Thank you, George. Now, if you'll mount up, we'll get the hell out of here."

Chapter Nine
Hammetsville, Texas
August 23, 1863

Travis had not spent a comfortable night. The evening meal served by Emma Crockett had been good, some of the best food he'd had in months. But as they sat there eating, and as she talked about the diary, he realized that he wasn't sitting there just because of the promise of Spanish gold. He'd been sitting there for any excuse he could think of, watching as the flickering of the firelight highlighted her high cheekbones. The lamplight reflected from her eyes, and Travis had to force himself to concentrate on something other than the top button of her dress that had worked itself free.

Crockett, on the other hand, seemed to be thinking only of the diary and the gold. She rarely mentioned her father, but Travis felt him in the room like another person. He was in the corner watching them, protecting his daughter. Travis tried to force his mind to the gold.

Finally she had stood and asked, "Where do you plan to sleep tonight?"

Travis shrugged but didn't speak.

"You can stay in here, near the fire, if you'd like," she said.

Travis thought about it. Thought about being in the same room with her and decided that he'd be safer outside. The temptation to say or do something he'd be sorry about would be too great if he stayed inside.

"I'll check my horse and the mule, and then spread my blanket outside."

"If that's what you want," she said shrugging. "Be more comfortable in here."

That hadn't been what he wanted, but it was what he had done. He had told himself that her invitation was nothing more than an act of kindness. He had told himself that she needed help to go for the gold, and that was the only reason that she wanted him to stay around. That was why she had invited him along.

So he'd gone outside, walked all around the cabin, studying the ground. That was something else he had learned in the army. Check the terrain in case the enemy arrived during the night. Be ready to fight or escape, depending on the situation.

Travis had spread his blanket but had not felt comfortable. Something was wrong, but Travis didn't know what it was. He had gotten up a couple of times and scanned the hills around the cabin. He searched for signs that someone was out there but couldn't see a thing. There were no camp-fires and there was no movement.

Just before the battle at Gettysburg he'd felt the same way. There had been nothing he could put his finger on at Gettysburg either. Just a feeling of impending doom. Maybe it was something he sensed in the air, or something that he had heard, or something that he believed. Now that feeling was back.

But the night had slipped away with no trouble. Travis had been awake through most of it. He had laid on his back, his hands under his head, and stared up into the night sky. He had watched as the moon had tracked through it, a bright white light that washed out some of the stars. And he had used the light as he had searched the ground around him without result. There was no enemy in the hills around him and he began to think that the sense of unease was the result of the woman sleeping no more than fifteen feet away. He hoped that she was having as rough a time as he was, and then hoped that she wasn't. She'd just lost her father. Sleep was the best thing for her. He wished her a quiet night with only the best of dreams.

Finally, it was morning and Travis had gotten up. He'd walked around the cabin again and then checked his horse. Satisfied that the beast had made it through the night safely, he had sat down on the wall and watched the cabin, waiting for Emma Crockett to let him know that she was awake and that it was time for him to come inside.

The door opened a few minutes later and she stood there, a hand raised against the sun. She was fully dressed. "You ready for some breakfast?"

Travis hopped off the wall and walked toward the door. "Of course. But then we've got to leave. It'll be a couple of days to El Paso."

"I'm ready now," she said. She stepped back and let him enter the cabin. "There's nothing here for me now. Not with my father gone."

"We won't be able to take much with us."

"I'll close the cabin. If we find nothing, I'll come back here. My friends will make sure that my things are left alone. If we find the gold, then I won't need any of it."

Travis shrugged. He pulled out a chair and sat down. She turned and began to work at the counter near the sink and the hand pump for water.

"You know," said Travis, "you could give me the information and the maps and I could go in search of the gold. You wouldn't have to leave here."

"I thought I made myself clear," she said, turning to face him. "There is nothing left for me here. I want to go. I have to go."

"Fine," said Travis. "It was just a thought."

She cracked the eggs into the pan, scrambled them with a wooden spoon, and then walked to the fireplace. She set the pan on a metal grate and shook the handle. She studies the fire and the eggs and didn't say anything else to him.

Travis had planned to ride out as soon as breakfast was over. He'd then revised the plan, telling her they'd take only what they needed to get to El Paso and then would buy any additional supplies there. But Emma Crockett didn't have a horse, just her father's mule. Travis ended up riding into Hammetsville to buy a buckboard and two horses to pull it. He returned to find Crockett waiting for him. She had dragged the chest out of the door and was sitting on it.

"We're not going to be able to take this all the way to the cave," said Travis, stopping close to the gate.

"Why not? The Spanish had their wagons close to it. It'll make it easier to get the gold out."

Travis wrapped the reins around the brake after setting it and dropped to the ground. He took a deep breath and thought about telling her to wait behind again but knew it would do no good. She was a strong-willed woman who had nothing to wait for in the cabin.

She stood up and moved away from the trunk. Travis grabbed the leather handles and lifted. The trunk was lighter than he would have expected it to be. He glanced at her.

"Just a few things I want to keep safe," she said. "The important things."

"I thought your friends would watch the cabin."

"They will." She retreated to the cabin.

Travis loaded the chest and shoved it toward the front. He turned as she came out of the cabin closing the door behind her. She carried a double-barreled shotgun and a revolver in a holster.

"My father's," she said.

Travis took the weapons from her and put them in the back, near the trunk. He then held out a hand to help her as she climbed up to the seat.

He walked around the back, made sure that his horse was ready, and then climbed aboard. He unfastened the reins. "If you're sure."

"Let's go."

Freeman was standing at the base of a tree, hidden in the shadows of it. He had an unobstructed view of everything that was going on below him. As Travis climbed to the seat far below him, Freeman turned to Crosby.

"They've got a wagon now."

"Which means?" asked Crosby sitting up and scrubbing at his face.

"It means that he's going to be moving slow and that the woman is going with him. We hang back and they'll take us to the gold. It means that they won't be running away from us."

Crosby stood up and moved to the tree. He stepped behind it as if afraid that Travis or Crockett would see him. He watched as the wagon moved down the road and into the small town.

"We follow them?"

"Hell," said Freeman, "that's the road to El Paso. A straight shot in. I figure they're going to El Paso. We'll just ride on ahead and wait for them there."

As the wagon disappeared among the low buildings, Crosby stepped out into the open. "What if they don't go straight to El Paso?"

"Then we backtrack and find where they left the road. It won't be that difficult to find them."

Crosby stretched and then reached down, opening his fly. As he relieved himself, he asked, "What are you going to do with your share?"

Freeman grunted and then shrugged. "Buy a whorehouse and stock it with the best whiskey. After a month or two, I'll come out and think of something else."

Crosby finished, shook his foot, and then buttoned up. "We going to eat breakfast first?"

For a moment Freeman stood looking down the ridge. At the far end of the town he saw the wagon reappear, heading for El Paso. It was obvious that Travis was in no hurry and that he didn't suspect anyone was behind him. He was taking it easy.

Freeman turned and moved down to where the fire was burning low. He'd let it die during the night so that no glow would be visible, even though on the reverse side of the slope, away from the cabin, there was no chance for Travis to scc it.

"Breakfast first," said Freeman. "Then we'll ride down, make sure they're still on the road, and then head on to El Paso."

"And wait."

"And wait," agreed Freeman.

Chapter Ten
El Paso, Texas
August 25, 1863

Travis met her in the lobby of the hotel. Her room was on the first floor and his on the second. The owner had seemed to be happier with them separated by that much space. Travis had wanted them on the same floor, in neighboring rooms, but she hadn't cared about the arrangement, so he let it stand. Now Crockett sat on one of the ornate couches with a high back and intricately carved feet. She glanced up, almost shyly, as Travis approached her.

"Now what?" she asked.

"I'm going to circulate and see what I can learn. Maybe hit a saloon or two and listen to the talk. See if there is anyone interested in Spanish gold or in Apaches. Especially in the Apaches."

"And war news," she said.

Travis shot her a glance. "Why the war news?"

"My brother is fighting in the war. He's with Robert E. Lee and the Army of Virginia."

Travis had heard that he had faced the Army of Virginia at Gettysburg. He thought of all the young men in gray uniforms killed as they tried to take Cemetery Ridge from the Federal forces. He thought of the dead men and the wounded men and young blood staining the sun-dried fields.

"I'll see if I can buy a paper," he said.

"Hurry back," she said, smiling.

Travis turned and walked out the door. El Paso was a busy town in the middle of the day. The sidewalks were crowded with people—men, women, and children. The streets were filled with horses and wagons. Men stood in knots outside the marshal's office, the newspaper office, and the saloons, talking. A few women stood close to the general store or the dry goods company. Kids, as always, were running around chasing one another or a stray dog or anything else they could find.

Travis stood there for a moment and then stepped into the street. He walked across to the newspaper office where the latest war news was tacked to a board near the door. It was the story of a battle, drawn in the broad strokes of a headline writer that told him nothing but were designed only to attract interest. For the details, a newspaper was needed.

And there was news from the territories all around them. Word of an Indian attack in New Mexico. A stage station burned and three people killed "most horribly."

But there was no talk of gold. No talk of the Spanish leaving their mark on Texas or the string of missions they built throughout the Southwest. Travis moved closer to the men and eavesdropped. They were more concerned with the way the war was going. The tides seemed to be turning with Lee's retreat from Pennsylvania. Some were afraid of an invasion from the North while others said that no Yankees would live to cross the border into Texas.

Travis turned and walked toward one of the saloons. Two men sat in chairs outside, watching the people walk by them. Another man sat at the edge of the boardwalk whittling. He was sharpening a stick, the shavings falling around his feet.

Travis walked into the saloon and saw half a dozen men standing at the bar drinking. There was a table pushed into a corner where another five men were playing cards. A single woman with light-colored hair stood behind one of the men, watching the game carefully.

He dropped a couple of coins on the bar and said, "Whiskey."

The bartender put a shot glass in front of him, filled it, and then backed off. Travis downed the drink in one swallow and slammed the glass back to the bar. "Again."

He took the drink and drifted toward the cardplayers. Travis knew that he had to be careful about where he stood. If any of the players thought that he could see their cards and was signaling to someone else, things could get ugly. He took a position near the stairs where he could listen to the bets and watch the players but where it would be nearly impossible for him to see any of the cards.

"You get me a beer, dear," said one of the players, turning to the lone woman. He reached out and ran a hand up the outside of her leg.

As she moved away, two men entered the saloon. Travis glanced at them, then away, and suddenly back at them. He recognized them immediately.

"Damn," he said. He drained the whiskey, looked around, and then set the glass on the stairs, pushing it over so that it was under the railing. Then, without looking, he ran up the steps, taking them two at a time.

He reached the top and walked down the hallway. One side was lined with doors but the other was open so that he looked down into the saloon. The two men had pushed their way to the bar and had both ordered whiskey. The bartender was standing close, a bottle in his hand.

They drank for a moment and then turned, looking around. Their eyes fell on the card game and they drifted toward it, watching as another hand was dealt.

"Hello," said a voice.

Travis turned and saw a woman standing in an open door. She wore very little. Her hair was tangled. She grinned broadly and touched herself between the breasts, drawing his attention to them. Travis tried not to look.

"You interested in some fun?" she asked.

"No."

"Then what you doing up here?"

Travis tried to look beyond her, into the interior of the room. He could see a bed that hadn't been made. There was a chest with a cloth on top of it and a china bowl with a pitcher inside it.

"Can I get out through there?"

"Now why would you want to do that?" she asked, grinning broadly.

"That's all I want right now," said Travis. "Can I get out that way?"

"You don't mind dropping off the top of the porch, you can get out that way."

Travis started to push past her but she grabbed his arm. "You go into my room it's going to cost you four bits."

"I just want to get out."

"Doesn't matter. You enter my room and it costs you four bits." She held out a hand, still grinning. "It's four bits if you walk right through and four bits if you stop for a few minutes for a little fun."

Travis looked into her eyes. Hard eyes. Unfeeling eyes. She didn't care what happened as long as she got her money. He dug in his pocket, found a coin and gave it to her. He held up another so that she could see it and said, "I was never here. You never saw me."

"I don't know what you're talking about. I haven't seen anyone in the last hour."

Travis nodded and dropped the coin into her palm. He closed the door behind him and moved to the window. As he reached it, he was aware of the odors in the room. It smelled like the inside of a lion's den after someone had sprayed it with perfume. It was dark in the room with the shades drawn. There were clothes on the floor. Shoes near the clothes. And there was a playbill hanging on the wall announcing a performance in the opera house in Denver.

Travis pushed the shades aside and opened the window. The air from outside seemed to be so fresh. He took a deep breath and then looked at the top of the porch. He climbed out, stood for a moment making sure that it wouldn't collapse under his weight. He moved to the edge, climbed over the waist-high railing, and dropped down to the back alley. There was rotting garbage piled in it. The odor of it, and from the outhouse off to the side, overpowered the stench from the stables close by.

Travis hesitated there, and then moved around the corner where he could look out onto the street. No one was paying him any attention. He slipped along the side of the building and then joined into the circulating crowds.

Looking back, he could see that no one had left the saloon. Another couple of men entered it, but no one came out. He didn't think the two men had spotted him. They had just wandered in for a drink. They hadn't looked up at him.

Travis hurried back to the hotel. He found Crockett sitting where he'd left her. She was staring out the window, not seeing much of anything out there. She was fanning herself with a piece of folded paper.

Approaching her, he said, "We've got a problem."

"Yes?"

"I saw two men I recognized. I saw them in Sweetwater."

"The ones who killed my father?"

Travis studied her for a moment. He knew what she was thinking. She'd want to turn them into the marshal, and then they'd be stuck in El Paso for weeks as they waited to testify against them. There was a chance that they'd be acquitted if their friends lived in El Paso. Back in Sweetwater, they might hang. In El Paso, they might be freed to walk the street looking for revenge. There was no percentage to accusing them in El Paso. Not since he was alone against two.

"No," he lied, feeling as if he were betraying a friend. A real friend. "They're not the ones, but they were around to hear the story of Spanish gold."

"You don't think it's a coincidence that they're here?"

Travis shook his head. "No. Your father spent an afternoon and evening spinning his stories of Spanish gold. A lot of men heard the stories."

"You think they followed us?"

"I don't know." Travis sat down next to her. He kept his eyes on the floor. "The marshal in Sweetwater told me where to find you but only because I said I'd take you father's possessions to you. No one else knew that. They'd have had to be on the trail to follow me and I didn't see anyone back there." His mind was racing as he tried to figure it all out.

But as he thought about it, he knew that it wasn't quite true. Someone had taken a shot at him almost in sight of Sweetwater. As he'd ridden toward Hammetsville, and then on to El Paso, he hadn't been looking for anyone following him. He'd done nothing to disguise the trail. Someone could have been following him and he might not have seen them, especially if they were trying to keep out of sight.

"Maybe it's a coincidence that they're here in El Paso," said Crockett.

"I'm not sure I believe in coincidence," said Travis. "At least not ones like this."

"There's not many places to go from Sweetwater."

"Northeast to Dallas or southeast to New Orleans," said Travis. "Lots more of interest in those two towns."

"Unless you've heard a story of Spanish gold," said Crockett.

"That's what I was thinking," said Travis. "El Paso is the perfect place to begin the search."

She looked at him, still fanning herself. "My father, if he could get someone to buy the whiskey, would keep talking. Hesitate with the money and he'd tell a little more so that the whiskey would continue to flow. He'd tell everything he knew in an evening if someone kept buying."

"So those men could easily know the general location and they'd know that El Paso was the starting point."

"I think so."

Travis rubbed a hand over his face. "Then what we need to do is get out of here now. Before they learn that you're here, too."

"No," said Travis, "but they might recognize me, and they know that I heard the story of the gold. We've got to lay low and get out tonight."

"There are things we need to buy."

Travis nodded. They'd planned on re-supplying in El Paso. But he hadn't counted on seeing others from Sweetwater. He knew that those two men were in the saloon drinking. If they hurried, they could get the supplies bought, have dinner in the hotel, and then ride out under the cover of darkness.

"No more than an hour," said Travis. "We get everything arranged in an hour and then meet back here."

She looked at him carefully and asked, "Are you sure those aren't the men who killed my father?"

Feeling like a jerk, he looked her right in the eye and lied to her. "They're not the same ones."

"One hour then," she said, standing.

Chapter Eleven
Outside El Paso, Texas
August 25, 1863

Davis had crawled forward to the edge of the bluff, and hid in the shadow of a huge boulder. Below him, in a box canyon, was a copse of cottonwood trees guarding a small pool of clear water. Around it were half a dozen Indians and their ponies. They seemed to be unconcerned that white men might be close. They seemed to care about nothing, other than drinking the water and letting their horses drink their fill.

Davis shoved himself back away from the edge and slipped to the rear where the others waited. He leaned close to Culhaine who stood holding a Winchester lever-action carbine.

"Apaches down there. Not doing much of anything."

"Except keeping us away from the water," whispered Culhaine. "That's all they've got to do."

"We could take them," said Davis. He waved a hand indicating the others with him. "Each man pick a target and we let fly. They'd be down before they knew what hit them."

"But the others would know," said Culhaine.

Davis was about to ask what others, but he knew. This small group had been detached to guard the watering hole. It was the only place in fifty miles that water could be found. Any white men in the region would have to swing by it for water and that would alert the Apaches about them.

"We need the water," said Davis. His mouth was filled with cotton and he was sweating heavily. There was water in his canteen. A little water. Just enough to get him through the night, but the next day would be hell without water, and he had none for his horse. Without his horse, he'd be on foot and the little water left would not be enough.

Kincaid slipped away from the main group and asked, "What's happening?"

"Keep your voice down," snapped Davis.

"There a problem at the water hole?"

"Hell yes," said Davis. "Six or seven Apaches are down there."

"We can take them," said Kincaid.

"That's not the trouble," said Culhaine. "We kill them and every Apache in the territory is going to know about it in a day, day and a half."

"We can't turn back now," said Kincaid. He pointed at the rest of the party, now grown to fifteen men. All were armed with repeating rifles, there were a couple of shotguns, and each man had one pistol and a couple of them had two.

"We can defend ourselves from any war party the Apaches can mount," said Kincaid. "We've got them out-gunned."

Davis wiped a hand over his face and rubbed the sweat on his faded flannel shirt. "I don't like this."

"Hell man," said Kincaid. "There's enough gold around for all of us for the rest of our lives. You said so yourself. Now you want to stop because there are some Apaches around the water hole."

Culhaine spoke up. "There's no reason to assume they're hostile. A couple of us could ride in and see what happens. The rest filter in among the rocks to protect us in case things go wrong."

"You want to do that?" asked Davis.

"Nope, but I don't see any way around it, except to just open fire from the rocks."

Davis stood there for a moment, thinking rapidly. The last thing he had wanted was to end up leading the party, but it was he who had heard the old prospector tell the story of the gold, and he was the one who knew the last piece of information for finding it. The others had naturally looked to him for the decisions as they had ridden across the desert.

"Culhaine, you and one volunteer will ride up to the water to see what the Apaches do. They let you water your horses and fill your canteens and ride out unharmed, then we'll send in another party."

"And if they don't?" asked Kincaid.

"We cut them down."

Culhaine nodded slowly and then said, "But don't let them have the first shot. They even look mean, you shoot them."

Davis wiped his face again. "Give us some time to get into position before you ride in. Who you going to take?"

Culhaine grinned and said, "Kincaid here. He's got a good reason to hate the Apaches."

"Now wait . . ." He realized there would be no way for him to talk his way out of it. He drew his revolver and checked it carefully. When he came to the empty chamber, the one normally under the hammer, he fed a fresh cartridge into it so that he would have all six shots before he had to reload.

"Jason?" said Davis.

"Damn, Will," he said.

"It was your idea."

"I know. I just don't trust those Apaches."

"They're supposed to be friendly now. Jeff Davis and his government has promised all the Indians their own homeland when the war is over."

Culhaine smiled weakly. "You think these Apaches know that? You think they care?"

"We'll be watching from the rocks. It looks like they're going to get trigger happy, we'll cut them down."

"Why do I keep wanting to say, 'Yes, sir,' to you?"

Davis clapped a hand on Culhaine's shoulder. "Because I was a lieutenant in the army for a while there. I inspire the men around me."

"Sure."

"Give us an hour," said Davis. "Then you ride in."

Culhaine gave in to the temptation. "Yes, sir."

As Culhaine walked back to where his horse was, Davis moved up the slope again. He paused next to a sun-hot boulder. Two of the others were breaking away from the main group, coming toward him. Both had their rifles.

"Wait here," he said.

Culhaine and Kincaid had separated their animals from the others and had climbed up into the saddles. They sat there for a moment and then wheeled around, riding back the way they had come.

The rest of the group began to filter up the slope. Davis shook his head and pointed at two of the men. "You stay back here with the animals," he said.

"Why?" asked one of them.

"Just in case. Suppose the Apaches have a couple of men running around out here. They could make off with the horses while we're occupied elsewhere. I want someone watching the horses."

"Why me?"

Davis stared at the man. He was one of the new men picked up on the trail. "What's your name?"

"Bradford. Sam Bradford."

"Well, Bradford, you stay down with the horses because I told you to."

"Who made you the boss?"

Bailey spoke up. "We did before you joined. You don't like it, ride out now."

Bradford faced Bailey, staring at him, his hand hovering near his gun. Then he smiled and said, "I guess that makes sense."

"There is more gold hidden out there than we can carry away in a year," said Bailey. "There is no reason to fight amongst ourselves."

Bradford and the other man retreated to where the horses were grazing. He sat down with his back to the rock where he could watch the ground all around him.

Davis turned and began the climb to the top of the ridgeline. As he approached it, he got down and crawled forward. When he could see down into the canyon, he stopped. The Apaches were two hundred, maybe three hundred yards away. Long shots but ones that could be made. No reason to risk exposing themselves to the Indians.

The men spread out along a line, using the cover that was available to them. Bailey crossed the ridge and slid down to an outcropping of the rock. He set his rifle down on the stone and pulled his pistol, checking it carefully. He set that next to the rifle, also on the stone to keep it out of the dirt, and then pulled back into the shadow to wait.

Davis kept his eyes on the Apaches. They sat around, talking quietly, and watching the trail that led up to the water hole. They didn't seem to have a care, and they didn't seem too worried about anyone arriving unannounced. It smacked of ambush, though he could not see the ambushers anywhere.

It was less than an hour later that Culhaine and Kincaid rode up. As they appeared at the far end of the canyon, the Apaches came to life. Two of them slipped up into the rocks directly below Davis and his men. They tried to hide, but Davis could see both of them easily.

Two others headed to the rocks on the other side of the canyon. Again, they hid but Davis could still see them. That left the two who remained by the water hole. They stood facing the approaching white men.

One of the Apaches held up his hand and stepped forward in a friendly fashion. Culhaine halted and sat there, looking down at the Indian. Neither man said a word for a moment. Kincaid reached back slowly, fingered his pistol and then let his hand fall away from it.

They began to speak, but the distance was too great, and Davis couldn't hear the words. It all seemed friendly enough with the second Apache, the one closest to the water, waving at them, gesturing them forward.

Culhaine slipped off his horse. He held the reins in one hand and began to walk forward. He kept his attention focused on the two Apaches that he could see.

Directly below, Davis watched as one of the Indians stood up, aiming his rifle. It was pointed right at Culhaine and Davis knew that the trap was about to spring. He raised his own rifle, aimed at the bronzed back of the Apache and began to squeeze the trigger.

Someone else fired first. The round struck the Apache in the shoulder, shoving him forward and down. He lost the grip on his rifle and it fell to the ground.

There was a second shot and then a third. An instant later there was a volley as everyone opened fire. The second Apache below in the rocks, was hit four times. He was shoved forward against a boulder, and then he fell, leaving a dark, wet smear on the rough stone.

A shot rang out from the other side of the canyon. Culhaine's horse screamed and reared back, kicking its front feet. It toppled to its side as Culhaine dived forward, out of the way. He rolled and yanked his pistol clear.

One of the Apaches leaped toward him, grabbing at his hand. Culhaine tried to jerk his hand and weapon away but the Indian seized it. He tried to stab Culhaine with his knife, but then twisted away as Culhaine pulled the trigger. The pistol fired but the bullet whined off harmlessly.

Kincaid leaned down, hugging the neck of his animal. He pulled his pistol and fired the six shots as quickly as he could. He hit one of the Apaches, driving him back toward the water in the pool.

The two Apaches opposite them continued to shoot. One round hit Kincaid in the side. He screamed once in surprise, and then rolled from the saddle. He lost the grip on his pistol, dropping it, but held onto the reins as his horse leaped back. Kincaid hit the ground, moaned, and didn't move.

Culhaine shoved at the Apache brave once. The Indian staggered and fell back. Culhaine swung his hand and fired his pistol. The round slammed into the Apache's face. Blood spurted as the brave fell to his back, his feet drumming in the soft sand.

Firing from the top of the ridge pounded the rocks on the opposite side of the canyon. Bullets whined off as the Apaches there tried to fight back. They popped up, fired, and dropped. But there were too many white men now, all shooting at the last two Apaches.

One of them was hit in the leg. He leaped back, out of one line of fire, but exposed himself to another. He was hit again, in the stomach. As he fell clear of the rock, another round struck him.

The last Apache shrieked once and leaped from cover. With his knife held high, he charged at Culhaine. Culhaine spun to face him raising his pistol, but before he could fire, the Indian was cut down. He fell back to the sand and didn't move. Culhaine got slowly to his feet, his pistol aimed at the downed Indian, and walked toward him.

Davis was up as the last of the Apaches fell. He began to work his way down to the canyon. Those around him did the same thing. One man broke off, checked the body of the closest Apache, and then stole the dead man's rifle.

Davis reached the canyon floor. He moved toward Culhaine. "You hit?"

"No." Culhaine wiped his face with his left hand. "No. I'm not hit."

Davis turned toward Kincaid. He was laying on his back, his horse's reins wrapped in his hand. His blood from the wound in his side stained the ground. He didn't move and his unseeing eyes stared up into the afternoon sun. His face was pasty white, waxy-looking in death.

Bailey appeared. "Apaches are all dead."

Davis took a deep breath. "I didn't want this," he said. "I tried to avoid a fight."

"Apaches wanted it," said Bailey. "They started it. Nothing we could do about it."

"Let's get our water and get out of here," said Culhaine.

"No," said Davis. "We've got to bury the dead first. All of the dead."

"Why?"

"Maybe, when these bucks don't reappear, and someone comes looking for them, they won't find the bodies. Might give us a couple of hours, maybe a couple of days. Time to get in, get he gold, and get out."

Bailey crouched near Kincaid's body. "I wonder if he's got a family."

"Why?" asked Davis.

"Be nice to send them some of the gold. He earned a share of it."

"Hell," said Davis. "We'll tell them where it is and let them get their own, if they want. He grabbed on to us. We don't owe him a thing."

"Except that he's dead and he died helping us," said Bailey quietly.

"The luck of the draw," said Davis, "and nothing more."

Chapter Twelve
El Paso, Texas
August 25, 1863

Buying the supplies had been far simpler than he thought it would be. El Paso was the jump off point for prospectors heading into New Mexico, Old Mexico, back into southeastern Texas, or north into the Guadalupe Mountains. Hundreds of men came through El Paso, all of them heading somewhere else so that those selling supplies were making a good living. That meant they had a large stock from which to choose.

The big problem was water. Barrels could be bought, and they could be filled. But water weighed quite a bit, and hauling it long distances in the desert just didn't work. It evaporated and seeped from the barrel and leaked out onto the ground. Still, with water holes separated by fifty and a hundred miles, sometimes taking water barrels was the only way to cross the desert.

Travis had a wagon and he had horses. They didn't need shovels or picks or a hundred other things that prospectors had to carry. Lumber to build a placer mine, or pans to tickle it from the river weren't necessary. The gold had been mined and smelted and was sitting there waiting for those who could find it and carry it away.

He arranged to pick up a couple of barrels and to fill them later in the afternoon. He arranged for grain for the horses and food for Crockett and him. He bought an extra rifle and extra ammunition. That was the sort of thing that could always be used, and if they found themselves stranded without money, they could trade the rifle and ammo for whatever they might need.

That done, he headed back to the hotel, watching the crowds carefully. There was still a group of men outside the newspaper office. They were standing around reading the latest headlines that had been brought in by rail. The latest war news. One boy ran along the boardwalk yelling out the headlines. A man stopped the kid, spoke to him for a moment, and then hurried across the street.

Travis stood silently for a moment wondering what the news could be. He wondered if General Meade had managed to find the Rebels again and if another big battle had taken place. Thousands of men on a field with nothing to do but shoot at one another. No reason for it except that one side wore gray and the other wore blue.

For a moment he felt guilty because he had deserted his friends. The cause wasn't important. The cause was never important. It was the friends who had counted on him to be there to help them. The only reason he'd stayed in the army as long as he had was because of his friends.

"No," he said out loud. A woman stopped and stared at him and Travis smiled at her. "Ma'am." He touched his hat and then hurried around her, back toward the hotel.

He entered and found Emma Crockett waiting for him. She was no longer wearing her dress but had changed into jeans, a flannel shirt, and had tucked her hair up, on top of her head. She was drawing a few stares from some of the proper ladies of El Paso. One stood near a door, a lace handkerchief in her hand, fanning herself as if she couldn't believe the effrontery of a woman appearing in public in pants.

Travis said to her. "Looks like you've outraged the local ladies."

"Mister Travis, if I'm going to go crawling about caves, riding in the desert, and climbing on rocks, I will do it in clothes designed for that purpose." Her voice was icy.

"I've no objections," said Travis holding up his hands in mock surrender.

The woman with the handkerchief snorted and then turned leaving the room. Travis watched her leave and then shrugged.

Crockett chose to ignore her. "You get everything?" she asked.

"Need to pick up the water barrels and have them filled and then we'll be ready to go."

Crockett stood up and retrieved the hat on the couch. "Then let's do it."

"I thought we'd wait until after dark."

"It'll be dark in about an hour. Take us that long to get the barrels filled."

Travis shrugged. He didn't like the idea of them maneuvering in the street in the daylight. Too many people around to watch them. Too easy to see them from the saloon.

"Well?" said Crockett.

Travis followed her out the door. He stopped long enough to survey the street but the two men who had been in Sweetwater were nowhere around.

"Let's do it," he said.

Freeman finished his beer and then moved toward the table where the men were playing poker. He reached into his pocket, felt the coins there, the silver dollars mixed in with half bucks and quarters, and then looked at the money on the table.

"You have room for another player?"

The man holding the cards looked up and said, "Always room for one more. We're playing table stakes here. We're not going to sit around while you try to find enough money to call a pot. You don't have the money when you sit down, it's tough."

"Table stakes it is," said Freeman, pulling a chair over. The legs scraped on the rough wooden floor. He dropped into the chair, dug in his pocket, and pulled the money out. He began to arrange it.

"Doesn't look like you plan to stay around long," said the dealer.

Freeman stared at the man and then turned. "Crosby. Hand me our stake."

Crosby moved closer but when he hesitated, Freeman said, "Give it to me now."

Crosby dropped a couple of half eagles and a double eagle on the table. Freeman pulled the gold coins closer and asked, "That sufficient?"

"That'll do just fine," said the dealer. "Gentlemen, the name of the game is five-card stud. One down and the others face-up. Nothing's wild and no one gets an extra draw."

With that he dealt the face-down cards around the table. He hesitated while a couple of players checked their hole cards. Freeman didn't bother with that.

The dealer flipped out the next series of cards and then looked at the man with a king showing. "Your bet."

"Two bits."

When everyone was in, they went around again. The king was still high and he made another two-bit bet. On the fourth go around a pair of tens appeared. That man bet half a buck and one of the others folded. Freeman finally peeked at his hole card, lifting the corner and bending down until he saw he had a queen there. Paired with the one showing, he had the high hand depending on the hole cards of the others.

When the bet came around to him, Freeman bumped it a quarter. That got in a look from the dealer, but he said nothing. The final cards were dealt and there was a pair of jacks showing, and the man with the tens now had a pair of eights to go with them.

"A buck," he said.

Freeman had a pair of queens showing. One man might have a straight and the man with two pair might have a hole card that would match either of his pairs, giving him a full house. But to Freeman, the three queens, the two showing and the one hidden, was the hot hand.

When the betting got around to him, Freeman said, "I see the buck and bump it a buck."

"He's got three queens," said the man with the two pair.

"Or," said the dealer, "he's got two pair queen high."

Freeman wanted to grin. The only man he needed to worry about had just revealed he had nothing in the hole. Not if he was worried about Freeman having three queens. When the betting got around to him again, he bumped in another buck. Only the dealer stayed in.

"Not going to let you buy a pot," he said. "I call." He dropped a silver dollar onto the table.

Freeman flipped his hole card up, showing the third queen. He waited as each of the men examined his hand and then reached for the money in the center of the table.

"We've got to go," said Crosby coming back.

"What do you mean?" asked Freeman.

Crosby hitchhiked a thumb over his shoulder. "They're here. Saw them in a wagon."

Freeman started to speak and then stopped. He put a quarter in the center of the table and said, "For the dealer. For the good cards. Thank you."

"You can't run out now," said the man who had once held the two pair.

Freeman turned and stared at him. When the man said nothing more, Freeman dropped the money into his pocket. He nodded once at the dealer and said, "Thank you all. I'm sorry to have to run like this."

At the front of the saloon he caught Crosby staring out the window. "Where'd they go?"

"On the wagon, down that way. She's dressed for the desert. Looks like they're pulling out now."

"I figured they'd stay the night and start out in the morning."

"Maybe they can't wait," said Crosby. "All that gold pulls awful strong."

"You get the horses," said Freeman. "I'll walk down there and see what's going on. If they're riding out tonight, we'll be ready."

Crosby grinned. "Damn. I had a very nice evening arranged with one of the ladies here."

"Can't be helped now," said Freeman. "Later, after we've got the gold, you can buy all the ladies you need."

"I need one now," said Crosby.

"The lady will wait, the gold won't," said Freeman.

Crosby nodded and then looked at the stairs. "I know," he said. "I just wish I could do both."

Chapter Thirteen
El Paso, Texas
August 25, 1863

The two men filling the barrels in the back of the wagon didn't seem to be in a hurry. They were filling buckets at a pump beside the building and then dumping them into the barrel. But they weren't moving very fast.

Travis sat on the wagon for a while, watching, and then decided that three could finish the task faster than two. He looked at Crockett and asked, "You up to pumping some water?"

"Sure," she said.

Travis jumped down, held up a hand and helped her down. He spotted a bucket sitting on the ground at the side of the building and walked over to pick it up. He turned it over, looked at the bottom, and then moved toward the pump. Emma Crockett was standing there, using the handle. She had gotten into the rhythm of it, and the water was splashing out into one of the buckets held by one of the men.

When he pulled the bucket clear, Travis took his place. He held it under the faucet, let Crockett fill it, and then turned, moving toward the wagon and the barrel. He lifted it up over his head and dumped it into the barrel, and then headed back to the pump.

Crockett was beginning to slow down. Sweat had beaded on her face, and she was breathing hard. She switched arms often, as the resistance to the pump's handle began to wear her out. She grinned weakly at Travis.

He dropped his bucket and said, "Let me do that."

She nodded gratefully and stepped away. "Feels like I'm pumping it up from China."

One of the men with the buckets grinned, showing his broken and yellowed teeth. "Had to dig deep to find the water. Had to dig real deep."

Travis waited until the bucket was set and began pumping away. When that bucket was full, the second man stuck his under and filled it.

After fifteen minutes they had both barrels filled and one of the men had fastened the lids to the tops of them so that evaporation would be slowed and they wouldn't be spilling water. Travis paid them and then climbed up.

"We going to eat here?" asked Crockett.

Travis shook his head. "I think we'll just get on out of town. We've got an hour of light left. Get us a good start on things."

She nodded.

Davis sat on top of a rock and watched as three of the men dug in the sand creating half a dozen shallow graves. Davis held a canteen in his hand and was drinking from it, surprised at how cool the water from the pool was. Normally the water in watering holes was tepid and sometimes it was warm because of the sun, but this was cool, almost cold.

That had to mean it was bubbling up from deep underground and that there was some kind of current in it that kept the water circulating. Davis found that mildly interesting but didn't see any significance in it. Except that the water was cold.

And then he thought, when he had his share of the gold, he could buy this land. It would be perfect for a little hotel, a stage stop, and a bar. Water to be purchased by the travelers. It would work on the order of the hot springs elsewhere. People traveled for days to get to hot springs. Why not for cold springs? Especially when it was the only water for fifty miles around.

It was an idea that he liked. A hotel, a gambling hall, and a stable. A small town that he would own. Davisville. Or Davisburg. That was it. Davisburg. He would be the mayor and he would own everything in it. Right here. Where the water was so cold.

"That's about got it," said Bailey. "Got them buried."

Davis stuck the cork back in his canteen and slid off his rock. He looked at the ground. There were a couple of rises where the Apaches had been buried, but no one would notice them unless he was looking for them.

"Got the ponies rounded up?"

"Four of them. Two ran off. We couldn't get near them."

"No matter," said Davis. He glanced at the others standing there. Two men leaning on their shovels and one man standing cradling a rifle. At the entrance to the canyon were two other men. They were there to keep the Apaches from sneaking up on them.

"Time to go?" asked Bailey.

"Yeah," said Davis. "We'll get out of here, put some distance between us and the dead, and then stop for the night. From now on we're going to have to be careful."

Bailey took off his hat and wiped the sweatband in it. He was about to say something. He looked at Davis and then decided against it.

Davis ignored him. Instead he walked over to where the horses were being held. He glanced at the men he didn't know. The men who had joined them on the trail as they had ridden from Sweetwater toward El Paso and then turned to the north.

"You have a problem?" he asked one of them. He had forgotten the man's name.

The man spit on the ground and then shot a glance at the unmarked grave of the man killed by the Apaches. "Should say some words."

"Why?"

"Man dies, someone should say some words. Only fitting for someone to say some words."

"I don't know any words," said Davis. "Saw too many men die back east and get left on the field. No one had time for words for them. No one had time to bury them. Kincaid knew the score when he joined."

"Not right," said the man.

Davis stared at him. It was the second time in a short period that someone had questioned his authority. It was the second time that someone who had joined them late had decided that Davis should be challenged.

"What's your name?"

"Webster."

"You can stay and say words or you can ride out with us. Now. But not both."

Webster spat again and then nodded. "No time for the words now."

Davis pushed past him, glanced into the faces of the others. Men who had spent the last three years in Texas or the territories, avoiding the war back east. They had dodged the fighting to stay out here where they weren't as likely to catch a bullet. A man could live for months in Texas and never see another human. Not like back east where armies maneuvered, looking for each other. These men had no right to question him.

"We mount up and get the hell out of here," said Davis. "Before the Apaches return."

The others followed suit, climbing into their saddles. Davis waited, then tugged on the reins, turning his horse. Without a word, he dug his heels into the horse's flanks and started toward the entrance of the canyon.

Freeman was afraid that Travis would see him and recognize him. He wanted to stay out of sight, inside a building, but he also wanted to see what Travis was doing. He wanted to be in a position to follow them as they left. It was now important that he stay close to them.

Crosby was standing right beside him. They were both standing in a general store, looking out the window. Crosby said, "They're taking a lot of supplies."

"All the better for us," said Freeman. "We'll be able to use those things once they've located the gold for us."

Crosby nodded but didn't say anything.

Freeman glanced back over his shoulder. There were two women in the store, looking at bolts of cloth imported from the East. A boy was looking at the candy jar sitting on the counter. The clerk stood there, his back to shelves filled with dry goods. Dungarees, shirts, blankets, and the like. Along another wall were canned goods. There were shovels, picks, saws, and axes. Everything that a man could need to start a homestead or to outfit a rig to head into the desert.

Freeman turned back to the window. The sun was slipping toward the horizon. The number of people on the street had diminished. They were heading inside for the evening meal. Chores that needed light had been finished. Now they were getting ready for the night.

"You think they'll leave now? Tonight?"

Freeman shrugged. "I'd wait until first light," he said. "But then, I'm not in a race."

"Meaning?"

"Hell, that man was there while the old prospector told us all about the gold. He knows that talk of gold gets people moving like nothing else can. He made his way to the daughter and now wonders who might be following. He'll want to get started as quickly as possible."

"Tonight?"

"Hell, you don't fill the water barrels and then let them set all night."

"So they're going tonight."

"Right," said Freeman.

Crosby looked at the others in the store, but they were busy buying their goods. No one was watching him or Freeman. Lowering his voice slightly, he said, "How we going to do this?"

"We'll just hang back and see what direction they go. We can catch them outside of town and follow them."

"Be easier if we knew where they were going to go," said Crosby.

"Of course," answered Freeman. "But I was right about this, wasn't I? They did come into El Paso just as we thought they would."

"So we let them lead us right to the gold and then take it away from them?"

"That about covers it."

Chapter Fourteen
North Of El Paso, Texas
August 25, 1863

The spot was perfect for a camp. Close to the road, but with enough cover that no one else would be able to see the wagon unless he came looking for it. A rocky shelter for the fire and protection from the wind if it picked up. As Travis climbed from the wagon, he saw the remains of a fire on the ground. Others had used the site in the past.

Travis walked around it slowly, checking it carefully. No rocks for snakes to hide under, no signs of scorpions or tarantulas. The ground was free from debris. The others who had used the spot had cleaned up after themselves, so that there was nothing left to draw insects or scavengers.

"We'll spend the night here," said Travis. "I'll unhitch the horses and get them fed and watered."

"I could start a fire," said Crockett.

"Fine. Just not too big." He grinned. "Though I doubt you'll find any firewood close by or enough to make a big fire."

"Why?"

"Somebody else will have already picked it up."

She shrugged. She moved around the rock and then began walking along, searching for firewood.

Travis unhitched the horses and lead them around behind the wagon. He got them some water and then opened one of the sacks of oats for them.

With the horses taken care of, he dropped back to the ground.

Crockett had found a little wood and dropped it at the point where the other fires had been built. "You're right. That's all I could find."

"Wait here," said Travis. He climbed up over on outcropping of rock and swept the area there. He picked up a couple of logs and dragged them over. He pushed them to the ground below and scrambled down after them. Using the ax, he cut them in pieces and then stacked them over the wood that Crockett had found.

Travis worked to get a fire started as Crockett crouched close to him. She watched him light the wood, shielding the tiny flame with his hands as it began to spread.

"There."

"What are we going to eat?" she asked.

"Beans," he said. He stood and moved to the wagon, found a pot and the beans. He prepared them, dumped them into the pot, and carried it to the fire, setting it in the center of it.

Grinning, he said, "Maybe not the tastiest of meals, but it will be filling."

She sat down on the sand and stared into the flames. She was quiet for a moment and then looked up at Travis. "What are you going to do with your share of the gold?"

Travis shrugged. "I haven't thought about it." He glanced at her and said, "When I heard your father talking about it, I didn't believe it. I've heard stories of lost treasures all my life and have never seen anything to prove that there are lost treasures."

"You've never told me exactly what happened to my father," she said.

"You never asked."

She nodded slowly and then said, "I'd like to know. Exactly."

Travis continued to stare into the fire. He was watching the beans. Finally he said, "I don't know exactly what happened. I found him in an alley."

"With two other men."

"With two other men," repeated Travis. They were trying to get him to give up the map."

"Which he didn't have," said Crockett.

"He told them he had it memorized. There was nothing written down."

"And you chased them away," she said.

"Well, when I stepped into the alley, they took off. Your father had been stabbed." He didn't tell her that he watched them stab her father, or that he had been wandering the streets without his pistol. If he'd had a weapon, he might have prevented the stabbing. He didn't want her to know how inept he had been.

He picked up a thin stick and stirred the coals of the fire. If he'd had his pistol, he could have prevented the death of the old man. But he had chosen to leave it because he'd used his pistol too often at Gettysburg. There he had killed men because they were wearing gray uniforms. He'd killed on order and had been sickened by it. He didn't want to have to kill again, and by leaving his pistol behind, he had managed to avoid having to kill, but someone had still died.

"You couldn't get a doctor?"

"No time," said Travis. "He told me to tell you, take his belongings to you, and let you know what had happened. No time to get a doctor. He knew that. Told me that there was no time to get a doctor."

"Why would they kill him?"

"I don't know," said Travis. "Maybe they were just trying to scare him. Learn where the gold was hidden and somehow it got out of hand. Gold does that. It makes people do stupid things."

She continued to stare at Travis. "Gold didn't do that to you."

"Maybe because I still don't believe it."

"Then why are you here?"

Travis shrugged again. What could he say. He was there because he had nothing else to do. He was there because he felt he owed the old prospector something because he hadn't stopped the men from stabbing him. He was there because Emma Crockett was a good-looking young woman who needed his help. He was there as a way of paying back the prospector. He hadn't been able to save him, but he might be able to save his daughter. There was no good answer to her question. Or at least no answer to her question that he cared to give her.

He reached out and pulled the pot of beans from the fire. He looked down into it and said, "Looks like dinner is ready." He used a wooden spoon to stir it.

She ignored that and asked, "What was my father saying? I mean, what did he tell the men about the gold?"

Travis set the pot on the ground. He rocked back so that he was sitting there, looking at her. "He was in a saloon getting the men to buy him drinks by telling them about the Spanish gold. He'd tell a little bit of it and stop until someone bought a drink. He told them everything including the fact that he had seen the gold himself."

"Did you see the two men there? Listening to his stories?"

"I saw them."

"Then you could recognize them," she said.

"If I saw them again, I would recognize them," he said.

She nodded and said, "Then we should find them and see that they are hanged. They murdered my father."

"Well," said Travis.

There was now steel in her voice. "They should be hunted down and jailed. They murdered a man."

"You don't want to let revenge color your thinking," said Travis. "It could turn you into a bitter woman."

"All I want is justice. Once we have the gold, we'll have the money to search for them." She looked up at him and said, "That's what I'm going to buy with my gold. Justice for my father."

Travis wiped a hand over his face. He reached out for the pot with the beans. They were still bubbling slowly. "That's a job for the marshal."

"My father was a gentle man. He might have told tales for free drinks, but what's the harm in that? It's no reason for two men to kill him."

"Those men could be anywhere now. A couple days ride and they're into desolate country. It would be impossible to find them," said Travis.

"So we shouldn't even try? Is that what you're suggesting here?"

Travis could tell that she was becoming angry. He said, "We'll try, but it shouldn't become a life's work."

"What else is there?" she asked. "Now?"

"There's getting married and raising a family."

"That an offer?" she asked suddenly.

Travis felt his stomach flip over. He didn't know if it was excitement at the prospect. Or the fear of it. "No. Just an alternative." He looked into the pot of beans again, suddenly not very hungry. He turned toward her and said, "I'm only suggesting that people who allow themselves to be consumed with a mission, no matter how right that mission might be, become something less than human." The image of the dead men at Gettysburg flashed through his mind.

"I don't need you to teach me about being human," she said. "You're little more than an opportunist, hanging on because I might be able to lead you to the gold."

"The gold isn't that important," said Travis, wondering if she would believe him. He kept his eyes on the beans, wondering if what she said was true. Was he there because of the gold, or was he there because he felt guilty about letting the old man get killed?

She laughed. "That's what everyone says. They don't believe the story and the gold isn't important, but the next thing you know, they're out there searching. Just like those men you saw in El Paso. Didn't believe Dad's story, but they were there just the same."

Travis sat quietly for a moment and then said, "I'm only here because you asked for my help. I still don't believe we'll find anything of value, even after seeing that diary. Just because it's a diary, it doesn't follow that it has to be true. Everyone assumes that what was written a hundred years ago, two hundred years ago, has to be true, but that man might have had a dozen other reasons for lying. Maybe he wanted people to settle in this region. Tales of gold would certainly spark the interest."

"Why would he want that?" asked Crockett.

"I don't know. Maybe the Spanish king had given him large tracts of land here and the only way he could make any money on it would be to get people to move into Texas so that the Spanish wouldn't try to take the territory back. Maybe he thought that getting people into the region would keep it all out of the hands of foreigners."

"Tomorrow," she said, looking right at him, "you can return to El Paso if you want. You're not required to follow me into the desert. I'll take care of this myself."

"And just how long will you survive out here by yourself?"

"I can take care of myself," she said. "I've been doing it since I was twelve years old."

"Living in a cabin at the edge of a town is different than surviving in the desert. If you don't know what you're doing, the desert will kill you. And if it doesn't, there are Apaches out there."

"The Indians are not hostile."

"The hell," said Travis. "If they want to do something, they're going to do it. They don't even need a reason."

"I said you're free to go."

Travis stirred the beans and lifted a spoonful to his lips to see how hot they were. Ignoring her last statement, he said, "We can eat now."

"Fine." She didn't speak for a moment and then asked, "What are you planning to do in the morning?"

Travis glanced at her and thought it would be very easy to leave her alone in the desert. He could ride into El Paso and have a good time. A little whiskey, a willing woman, and then out on the trail again.

But he just couldn't leave Crockett. He still felt he owed it to the old prospector to stick it out. He had to protect the old man's daughter. A week, ten days would be all that it would take before she was tired of the desert. It didn't take the desert long to sap the strength of the unwary. It had chased strong men out in less than a week. It had killed strong men in a day.

"If you don't mind," he said. "I'll stay with you until we either find the gold or abandon the search."

"The gold is there," she said.

"Sure," said Travis. "Sure it is."

Chapter Fifteen
North of El Paso, Texas
August 26, 1863

Travis woke just as the dawn was beginning to break and there was a streak of red orange across the eastern sky. He sat up suddenly, as if he thought the enemy, the Rebels, were approaching. He had not awakened so quickly and so alertly since he had opted out of the army and left the fields of Gettysburg far behind him.

He stood up and moved around the giant rock where he could look out on the road. There was nothing on it. Nothing around it. Nothing anywhere to wake him. Just something in the air that made him uneasy. An odor or a sound that was below the level of perception. Something that was there but at such a low level that he wasn't consciously aware of it. Something frightening that he couldn't see.

He walked back and looked down at Crockett. She was lying on her side, her eyes opened. "What is it?"

"Nothing," he said. "Be full light here in about thirty minutes or so."

"You want to get started?"

"It'll give us all day for travel. We can put a lot of miles in if we get started early enough."

She threw the blanket off and sat up. She was wearing a light cotton shirt and dungarees. They looked to be molded to her body and Travis found himself staring at her. He pulled his eyes away.

"There enough time for coffee?"

Travis looked down at the fire. It had burned itself out during the night. "It'd take an hour to find the wood and get the fire going. Let's just move on."

She moved to the wagon, climbed into the back, and took the lid off one of the water barrels. She dipped a hand in and took a drink. She then leaned over, her face only inches from the water, and splashed it up onto her cheeks and forehead.

"What in the hell are you doing?" snapped Travis.

"Washing my face."

"That water is for drinking and for cooking. It is for the horse and for us and has to last us while we ride around in the desert. It is not for bathing."

She stood up, her face dripping. "I was just washing my face."

"In the desert, it is a luxury that you cannot afford."

"When'd you become such an expert on the desert?" she asked.

"I'm just using common sense. Water is in short supply, so you don't waste it."

"Fine. I won't wash my face." She slammed the lid back onto the top of the barrel.

"At the water holes," said Travis. "That's different. Plenty of water there. But we have to be careful so we don't run out between here and the water hole."

"All right," she said. "I understand." Her face was an angry mask.

"What the hell's wrong with you?" he asked, surprised by her sudden anger.

"Nothing. I just don't need lectures. I didn't waste that much water."

Travis realized that the argument was no longer about wasted water. There was something else going on that he didn't quite understand. He looked away from her and her wet face and mumbled, "Sorry."

"Sure," she said.

"No, really," he said. "I'm sorry." He walked away then and began getting the horses ready to hitch to the wagon. He moved one around and backed it up toward the front of the wagon. He pulled at the leather harness, threw part of it over the animal's back, and worked to buckle it to the tongue. Finished, he repeated the process with the other horse. Then he made sure that the reins were clear, running his hands along them and finally tying them to the brake handle.

When he finished, he saw that Crockett had picked up the blankets, folded them, and tossed them in the back of the wagon. Without a word to Travis she climbed up and sat down.

Travis stood there for a moment, looking around. The fire was out and there was nothing left behind to show that they had been there. He then got up on the seat beside her, untied the reins, and shook them so that they rippled across the backs of the horses.

They pulled out from behind the rocks and then angled toward the road.

"North from here," she said.

"I know that."

"Then just follow the road."

Bailey rode closer to Davis and said, "I think there is someone behind us."

Davis turned in the saddle and scanned the horizon to the south. The land was open and there didn't seem to be anyone there. No sign of riders.

"Who?"

Bailey kept his eyes forward and said, "Apaches. Been there since last night."

"You sure? I don't see anything."

"And you won't unless they want to be seen." He fell silent and watched the ground at his horse's feet. "Apaches know what happened to their men at the water hole."

"You can't know that," said Davis.

"I can feel it," said Bailey.

Davis turned and faced the other man. He knew Bailey as a merchant. Not someone who had the second sight. Not someone who had a feeling for Apaches or understood them.

"I'd like something a little more tangible," said Davis.

"They're out there," said Bailey. "When you can't see them, it's when they're there."

"Crap," said Davis. "If you can't see them, it means you can't see them. It doesn't mean they're spooks able to appear and disappear at will."

"I know they're following us." Bailey still didn't look up at Davis. "We're leaving enough signs that an old lady in a wagon could follow us."

"If you want to ride on back to Sweetwater, I'm sure that no one will object. If you're scared, that is."

"No," said Bailey. "The last thing we can do is split up. We do that and they'll take us one at a time. Whittle us down until we won't be able to defend ourselves."

"Damn, I don't like the way you're talking," said Davis.

"I'm just saying what's true. Apaches are back there, dogging our trail, waiting for a chance to jump us. We need to find a place to defend."

"Cave's the perfect place," said Davis. "Gives us cover and limits the direction the Apaches can take to get at us. We'll just have to press on."

"Maybe if we turned around," said Bailey, "they'd leave us alone. If they think we're going after the gold, they might just jump us."

Davis took off his hat and wiped the sweat from his face. He put his hat on carefully. "You want to head back," he said again, "you go right on."

"Not alone."

"Then just shut up. I don't want to hear any more of this talk about them being out there. Keep it to yourself."

Bailey nodded and said, "Thought you'd want to know."

"I don't want to know. If you just feel them out there, you keep it to yourself."

Bailey spurred his horse and galloped off to the front of the short column. He slowed there and fell in behind Webster. Davis watched him go and then turned in his saddle. Again he scanned the ground behind them. Nothing there to suggest that the Apaches were following. Nothing to suggest there was anyone back there.

Settling down, he wondered if Bailey might not be right. The Apaches had to know that their men at the watering hold were dead. And they wouldn't have to be very good to be able to follow the trail. Davis and his men had done nothing to hide it.

Now Davis rode forward quickly. He slowed near Culhaine. "I think we'd better start watching our back trail."

"There a reason for that?"

"Apaches are going to be looking for the men who killed those bucks. They shouldn't have trouble following us."

"Thought we buried the bodies to prevent that."

Davis nodded. He felt light-headed, as if he'd been dipping into the whiskey too often and drinking it too fast. He wished, for that moment, that he was back in Sweetwater where everything was cut and dried.

"I just want to be ready in case."

Culhaine nodded and reined his horse around. He rode back the way they had come and then halted. He sat there waiting to see if anything moved near the horizon.

Davis watched Culhaine for a moment and then turned. Suddenly he was worried about the Apaches all because Bailey had a feeling.

"Damn," he said.

Freeman stood at the top of the ridge, his hand out against a rock so that it looked as if he was holding himself up. Far below him on the desert, he could see movement. The wagon was obvious. The horses were a dark brown against the lighter brown, the tan of the desert.

Off to the right, at the very limits of his vision, was another group of riders. He couldn't make out who they were or even exactly how many there were. Maybe a dozen. Maybe a couple more.

Crosby was kneeling next to him, holding the reins of both their horses. He was watching the wagon as it followed the road to the north.

"I told you they'd be easy to find," said Freeman. "They're heading toward the gold now."

"Who's that off to the right?" said Crosby.

"Probably some of the others who heard that old man shooting his mouth off."

"You think they're following the wagon?"

Freeman turned his attention to the horsemen. There was something wrong with them. Something about them that he couldn't quite place. He watched until they disappeared, riding over a ridgeline. He then looked back at the wagon. It didn't seem to be in a hurry.

"Doesn't look like they're following the wagon. Looks like they know where they're going."

"We going to head out?" said Crosby.

Freeman watched as the wagon climbed a slight hill and then reached the crest. A moment later it vanished. "Now we go," he said.

Crosby handed Freeman the reins for his horse and then swung up into the saddle. Freeman stood for a moment, searching the desert to the right. The riders who had been there had not returned. Now there was nothing moving anywhere on the desert except for the dust devils being stirred by the hot winds blowing from the south.

"We going?" asked Crosby again.

Freeman nodded but still watched the horizon to the east. He wished that he had gotten a better look at the riders there. He wished that he had been able to identify them.

"Yeah," he said. "We're going."

Chapter Sixteen
The Deserts of West Texas
August 26, 1863

The horses were becoming uneasy. Their nervousness was getting to Travis. They were approaching the box canyon that held a water hole, and there was something about it that bothered the horses. Normally, horses could smell the water and Travis would be hard pressed to hold them back. Now he was having trouble getting them to move forward.

Crockett picked it up, too. "What's the problem here?"

"I don't know," said Travis. He stopped the wagon and set the brake. The entrance to the canyon was a couple of hundred feet in front of them. There were wagon tracks, footprints, and a well-beaten path that lead into it. The rocky walls rose on either side of it and through the entrance, Travis could see the copse of green trees.

He handed the reins to Crockett and said, "I'm going to check this out. You wait here."

"And if you don't come back?" she asked.

"Then all the gold is yours, if you can find it." He jumped from the seat and then pulled his lever-action Winchester out. He walked forward and stopped near the horses. He reached up and patted one of them on the neck and then resumed walking into the canyon.

He kept his eyes moving, searching the rocks around the entrance, fearing an ambush. The Apaches sometimes did that, but so did the white man. Everyone knew that travelers would stop off at the watering hole. It was a good place for robbers, both white and red.

He thumbed back the hammer of the rifle. Behind him he could hear the horses snorting and pawing at the ground. There was a light breeze blowing and as he approached the canyon, he realized that it wasn't a fresh breeze. There was an odor on it. An odor that he recognized from his service in the army. It was an odor that hung over battlefields in the days after the fighting was over. He recognized it from the times that he had dug graves for the dead.

He stopped and turned back, looking at Crockett and the wagon. She was sitting there holding the reins and had one foot up on the brake. The horses were making her nervous.

He started forward again, slipping to the right so that he was in the shadow of the rocks. He reached the entrance, stopped, and crouched. Now the stench coming from the box canyon was almost overpowering. The last thing he wanted to do was move forward into it.

Finally he stood, his back to a boulder. He slipped around it until he was in the canyon. To the right, near the foot of the slope, were two big turkey buzzards. One had its head down and was tugging at something buried in the sand. The other was flapping around, trying to get in closer. He glanced up overhead and saw twenty or thirty vultures circling.

Opposite the one grave, he saw there were a couple more. There were buzzards clustered around another. They had it covered so that he could tell nothing about the body. He walked to the center of the canyon, but none of the vultures or buzzards took off. They sat quietly watching him.

Travis raised the rifle and fired a single shot. The sound echoed around as the birds leaped into the air; calling noisly. They joined the others circling overhead, waiting to see what would happen next.

Travis took in the scene. There were four dead men partially exposed. All seemed to be Apaches killed recently. The desert heat and the scavengers were already working on the bodies, turning them into bloated corpses that stunk.

For a moment Travis stood there, trying to figure out what it meant. He took a step forward and then stopped. He glanced at one body and then the other. Finally he walked to the closest one and then, holding a hand over his nose and mouth, knelt.

The dead man had a bullet hole in the side of his head and another in his chest. There were rusty stains near each hole, which was the dried blood. The skin was ripped in other places. That was where the birds had been picking at it. There were no fingers on the right hand.

There had been a fight in the last day or two. The dead Apaches, partially buried, meant that the winners had been the white men. It meant that other Apaches were going to be on the warpath. They would not allow several of their fellows to be killed without trying to get even.

"What is going on?" said Crockett suddenly.

Travis spun and saw her standing in the entrance to the canyon. Her eyes were on the dead man.

"I heard a shot," she said. "Did you kill him?"

"No," said Travis. "I fired to frighten the vultures. He was dead when I got here."

Now she saw the others. "What happened?"

"Looks like they got into it with some of our people . . . "

"Our people?"

"White men. Some kind of fight and they lost. Means there's going to be some hostiles out here."

"How's that going to affect us?" she asked. She was staring down at the dead man as if she had never seen anything so fascinating.

Travis shook his head. "I don't know. These guys were buried for a reason. I think that was to hide the bodies from the Apaches, for the little good it would do. I think the Indians are going to be out looking for who did this."

"Which couldn't have been us," said Crockett.

"Which won't mean a thing," said Travis. "If they decide to hit the warpath, then anyone with a white skin is going to be a target."

"You saying that we should give it up?"

Travis was silent for a moment. Then he shook his head. "Right now I think we can press on. We've seen no sign of any hostiles and until we do, I'm not going to worry about it. We might have to pack it in later."

"But the gold," she said.

"Will still be there next year after the excitement dies down. The gold will do us no good if we're dead."

"We're not turning back now?" she asked.

Travis looked at the dead men again and knew what the answer should be. Good sense dictated what it should be. But instead he said, "Not yet. I still want to see the gold."

* * *

"They're out there," Bailey said again. "I know they're out there."

"You see them?" asked Davis again.

"This time I've seen them," said Bailey. "Maybe a dozen of them. Maybe more. But I'll bet you my share of the gold that there are others I haven't seen. Apaches are like that."

Davis felt his stomach grow cold. It had been one thing to kill the Apaches at the watering hole. That had been an ambush where the Indians had been caught cold. Now it looked like the tables were about to be reversed.

Culhaine had seen a couple of the braves as they topped a ridgeline. He rode closer and said, "They're about three, four hundred yards to the west." He didn't want to point, afraid that would draw attention to himself.

Davis turned and looked in the opposite direction. He now understood why they had been allowed to see the Apaches. There was nothing but flat, open ground as far as they could see. No hills covered with rocks to provide protection. No rivers to cross so that the Apaches would have to attack across the water while they hid, picking them off. Nothing for them to defend except open ground.

Now there was a group of riders paralleling them. Davis watched them for a moment. Then, suddenly, ahead was another group.

"I think this about tears it," said Davis.

"What are we going to do?" asked Culhaine.

"They're forcing us to the east," said Davis. "No cover there yet. But if we can get a good run, maybe we can find something."

"When?" asked Bailey.

"We turn to the east," said Davis, "and continue to move in that direction. If they make a turn toward us, we get the hell out of here."

"Okay."

Davis turned in his saddle slowly and looked at the band of Apaches. They seemed to have something in sight, in front of them. They didn't seem to be interested in the group of white men who happened to be riding in the same direction.

"Slowly," said Davis. "Slowly, we turn to the east. Ramsey, you slide off to the right as a flanker. George, you and Jason drop back for a rear guard."

"They'll roll right over us."

"If they get close to us, stop, fire a few rounds and then turn and run. Buys us a minute of two," said Davis.

"Okay," said Bailey.

"Here we go." said Davis. He pulled on the reins and his horse's head turned to the right. He kept the pace slow, as if it was just a natural turn. Nothing important. He wanted to look back at the Apaches, but didn't want them to know it. He forced himself to keep his eyes to the front.

"They're turning with us," said Ramsey.

Now Davis glanced to the north where the second group had appeared. They, too, were headed toward the white men. No one was moving very fast, but it was now obvious that the Apaches were going to keep them in sight.

"I think it's time to make a run for it," said Ramsey.

"So do I," said Davis. He stood up in the stirrups and twisted around. He put on hand on his horse's rump and then watched the Apaches. They were following slowly.

"Men," said Davis raising his voice slightly, "I think it's time for us to scram." He dropped back into the saddle, touched a hand to the Colt revolver strapped to his waist and then, suddenly, kicked his horse in the flanks.

"Yeah!" he screamed and hunched forward as the horse jumped. It began to gallop across the desert.

The men with him did the same. Bailey and Culhaine hesitated, just for an instant so that they were at the rear of the formation. As they began to gallop, the Apaches to the north let out a whoop. They began to cut toward the white men, hugging the necks of their ponies.

"They're coming," yelled Bailey.

"Let 'em," said Davis. He was now watching the ground just in front of his horse, searching for a hole the animal might step in. The last thing he wanted was to be spilled to the desert floor while the Apaches rode down on him.

He lifted his eyes and swept the horizon. There was a single tree in the far distance, but that offered no hope of sanctuary. A single tree would do nothing except provide shade for them during the fight.

"Getting close on the right," yelled Bradford.

Davis glanced, but the Apaches were still three hundred yards away. They didn't seem to be gaining on them at all. Kicking up clouds of dust and screaming, but not catching them.

There were three shots from the rear. Davis shot a glance over his shoulder. Bailey and Culhaine were sitting there, aiming at the Apaches coming at them from the west. Those Indians slowed, and when they did, both men whirled and kicked their horses, joining the fleeing group.

"Where?" yelled Webster.

Davis knew that he wanted to know where they were going. Davis didn't have an answer. He hoped that reaching the slight rise in front of them would open things up. That over that rise would be a defensible position.

There was a distant shot. One of the Indians shooting at them. No one was hurt. The round disappeared harmlessly. There was a second and third, but Davis knew that a galloping horse made it impossible to aim.

They reached the top of the rise, and Davis reined in his horse. It stopped running, digging in its rear feet, sliding to a halt. The desert stretched in front of him like a lumpy blanket spread for a picnic. Nowhere to hide.

He turned and looked at the Apaches. They were now two hundred yards away and coming fast. The horses were breathing hard from the run. It would be an hour, maybe less, before the horses were run into the ground, unable to move. A horse would run until it collapsed, but once it was down, there was nothing to be done for it and no way to make it get back up. It would die where it fell.

Davis rubbed his lips with the back of his hand. His options were suddenly limited. Twenty, maybe thirty Apaches coming at him. He had ten, eleven, a dozen men, all with rifles and pistols. With nowhere to run, nowhere to hide, there was nothing he could do but stop and fight.

"Dismount," he ordered like he was still an officer in the Rebel cavalry. He jerked his carbine from the scabbard on the side of his saddle. He held the reins in his left hand as he worked the lever, putting a round under the hammer.

Around him the others did the same. Bradford, Bailey, and Culhaine handed their reins to Webster and then ran forward, kneeling or throwing themselves down on the ground, aiming at the Apaches.

"Take them," said Davis, snapping out the words like an order on a battlefield.

There was a single shot and then a volley. One Apache tumbled from the back of his horse, but the others came on, screaming and waving their arms.

Davis fired once, worked the lever ejecting the spent round, and pulled the trigger again. There was a rattling of the weapons around him and he thought suddenly of fire discipline. They should space the shots so they all didn't empty their weapons at the same time. Work it so there was a continuous fire pouring out. That would stop the Apaches.

But it was too late for that. He didn't have the time to instruct them in fire discipline. Not with them blazing away as fast as they could. Instead, he aimed at the closest of the Apaches and tried to kill him.

Two more of them toppled from their horses. One pony reared suddenly, unseating the rider. As the animal fell, the Indian was on his feet, but now he was aiming at the white men. Firing his rifle at them.

"Closest first," yelled Davis. "Kill the closest first. Aim for the horses."

"I got that one," yelled Bailey. "I got that one."

The Apaches suddenly veered to the right and then turned, riding toward the north. Davis followed them with the barrel of his rifle. He aimed, fired, but hit nothing. The Apaches kept riding away.

Now there was only the single Indian, standing on the desert about three hundred yards away. He had slipped to one knee and was using a short cactus for cover. He was firing at them slowly.

"Get that bastard," yelled Culhaine.

"Let's get out of here," said Davis. He started to jam his rifle into the scabbard and then stopped. He began pushing shells into it, reloading it just in case the Apaches decided to attack again.

Finished, he climbed into the saddle. Culhaine was standing, aiming at the Apache. He fired and a piece of the cactus exploded. There was no return fire now.

"Let's get out of here now!" shouted Davis. "Come on." He reined his horse around and started off toward the east again, this time at a trot.

The men mounted up and fell in behind him. As they crossed the rise and started down the gentle slope, Davis said, "We've got to practice fire discipline. If they come back we have to make sure that we don't all run out of ammo at the same time."

"They'll be back," said Bailey.

"Yeah," agreed Davis. "I know, and that's what I'm afraid of now."

Chapter Seventeen
The Desert North Of El Paso
August 26, 1863

Freeman and Crosby came up to the top of a ridge and looked down into the next shallow valley. At the far end of it was the wagon. Crosby sat there for a moment and then turned to look right at Freeman.

"I know where they're going."

"What?" said Freeman.

"Now that I see where we are, and the direction they're taking, I think I know where that old man was talking about. There's a shallow river about ten miles from here. North of the river is a cluster of mountains. That's got to be where they're headed."

"You sure?" asked Freeman.

Crosby closed his eyes and was quiet for a moment. He then opened them and nodded. "I know exactly where he was talking about. We don't have to follow them."

"Then let's go," said Freeman.

Crosby held up his hand. "They're bearing to the east here, but we can cut across the desert and cut four or five miles off the trip."

"I'll follow you," said Freeman.

Crosby pulled his horse around and then started down the slope. The horse picked its way around the clumps of prickly pear and the peyote and the wiry prairie grass. Some of the ground was soft sand, and other areas were as hard as rock. Once they reached the valley floor and could no longer see the wagon, they began to move faster. They rode around a copse of trees that seemed to mark a water hole, but when they got near they found nothing other than the cracked earth of a hole gone dry. There was the body of a horse near it.

"Now we turn to the northeast. We'll have to cross that ridge there, but then everything opens up until you get to the mountains."

Freeman didn't say a word. He turned his horse and began the long, gentle climb to the top of the ridge. An hour later they had reached it. The land fell away from them and was washed out in the bright sunlight. Far away, barely visible, was the dark shape of the mountains. It looked as if the mountains were across a shallow lake. The heat was shimmering on the sand, giving it the look of water.

"There," said Crosby, his voice higher. "That cave has it be over there. In those mountains." He grinned at Freeman. "It has to be."

Freeman sat there, studying the scene. "It does look like what the old man was describing."

"Not like it," said Crosby. "Is. Has to be." He stopped talking for a moment. "When I was a kid, I heard stories about this. Jim Bowie and a group of his friends found a cave and defended it from the Indians. They talked about a fabulous gold mine hidden in the desert."

"Bowie never got this far west," said Freeman.

"How do you know?" asked Crosby. "He got all over Texas and Mexico. You don't know where he might have ridden during those times."

"Doesn't matter," said Freeman, "if you're sure this is the place."

"We're close," said Crosby.

"Then let's get it over. Freeman was about to head down when movement to the west caught his eye. He turned toward it and saw a dozen riders come over the ridge.

"Looks like we've got company," said Crosby.

Freeman didn't move. He studied them and then said, "I don't like this. Not at all."

Then, to the south of the first group, a second appeared, and as Freeman turned he saw a third. All of them seemed to have a single destination in mind. All were angling, more or less toward the mountains directly in front of Freeman and Crosby.

"What do you think?" he asked.

Freeman shrugged. "I think we'd better head on down there as fast as we can. I don't want to get left out of this. Could be someone else who figured out the old man's clues."

Crosby kicked his horse and it started to move. He slapped the flanks with the ends of the reins and it began to gallop. Freeman followed him. Both men were riding fast now. Down the gentle slope to the valley floor and then north to the mountains.

Freeman was aware of the other riders angling north. Everyone seemed to be headed toward the same place. The only thing he wanted to do was reach the river, cross it, and get into the mountains before the other men could catch up or beat them there.

"Go!" he yelled at Crosby as he rode by him. "Let's go."

Crosby tried to get his horse to run faster. He was falling behind slightly. He risked a glance at the closest group of men and was shocked to see that they were not white.

"Apaches!" he yelled.

At first Freeman seemed not to hear. Then slowly, he turned to look. The wind caught his hat, blowing it from his head. He didn't stop to retrieve it.

"We make the river, we'll be okay," he called.

Turning to look back over his shoulder, he saw the second group closing on them. They were Indians, too. Maybe a dozen of them. Maybe more.

"Damn," he yelled. "They're catching us."

Freeman lowered his head so that it was near the neck of his racing horse. He stood slightly in the stirrups so that the constant pumping rhythm of the running animal wouldn't keep jarring his spine. Now the only thing he could think of was the shallow river. If they could reach that, they would be safe. Somehow he equated the river with safety. Nothing else mattered to him.

The desert opened up in front of him. Nothing to hide them. Nowhere to go. Just the wide open space until they reached the mountains. If the Indians caught them before they reached the mountains, they were as good as dead.

There was a shot behind him and Freeman risked a glance. Crosby had his revolver out. He'd fired it, pointing it to the rear but hadn't tried to aim it. Maybe he thought the sound would frighten the Apaches.

"Save your ammo," yelled Freeman. "You won't hit anything anyway."

Crosby squeezed off two more shots. The Apaches fired back. Three rounds and then a war whoop. They were screaming as they began to close on Freeman and Crosby.

Freeman was about to give it up. They wouldn't be able to outrun the Apaches. The only thing he could hope for was fighting it out and getting killed before the Indians captured him. Let them mutilate his dead body. He wouldn't care then. But he didn't want them to start the mutilations while he was still alive. They could make it last for hours, and that thought frightened him to the core of his soul.

"There!" screamed Crosby. "Over there."

Freeman shot a glance to the north where before, they had only been able to see the mountains. He saw horsemen there, too, but they didn't look like Indians. They looked like white men.

Freeman turned toward them immediately. Suddenly the gold wasn't all that important. All the gold in the world would do him no good if the Apaches caught him. With enough men with rifles, they could fight off the Indians. They would have a chance to survive.

"Get to them," said Freeman. He now looked at the first group of Apaches. They were angling in, but it didn't seem they would cut them off. There were more whoops and a couple of shots. Nothing that came close.

Turning, Freeman caught a glimpse of a shallow stream. There were trees along the banks of it. Bushes and plants. That had to be the river the old man had talked about. Had to be. They had stumbled onto it, and now the information would do him no good.

They rode along the river and then came to a place where the bank was no more than two feet higher than the surface. Freeman wheeled his horse and it leaped into the water. It stumbled but didn't fall. Freeman looked to the rear. The Apaches were catching them.

"Come on," he yelled and then ducked, hanging onto the neck of the horse.

They splashed across the river. The horse leaped at the far bank and lifted itself out of the water. Now Freeman slipped from the saddle. As he did, he drew his rifle from the scabbard, used the lever to cock it, and aimed at the Indians on the far bank.

He knelt in the soft sand as Crosby struggled across the river. As soon as he made it, Freeman was up. He swung himself into the saddle and jerked the horse around, digging in his heels. The animal began to run again.

Behind them the Apaches had reached the river, but they had stopped there. There were a couple of random shots that weren't well aimed.

"If I didn't know better," Freeman yelled at Crosby, "I'd say we're being herded."

Crosby didn't answer. He kept his head down and his rifle aimed at the other riders, now no more than five hundred yards away.

And then, beyond them, Freeman spotted another group. It looked as if the Apaches were herding everyone in one direction. Get them all in the same place and then eliminate them all at once.

Freeman reined in his horse. He stopped long enough to see that the Apaches had yet to cross the river. He then saw that behind them were even more Indians. Every Apache in the desert was riding down on them.

Crosby pulled up next to him. He wiped the sweat from his face on the sleeve of his flannel shirt and glanced to the rear. "What do you think?"

"I think we've stepped into it this time," said Freeman. "I think we're into it deep."

Chapter Eighteen
The Desert North of El Paso
August 26, 1863

The rifle shots echoed through the valley. Travis halted the wagon and turned his head, trying to pinpoint the shooting. He thought that it came from the west.

"What's that?" asked Crockett.

"Someone firing," he said. Not many men firing. Maybe a dozen or two and not shooting as fast as they could but firing faster than they would if they had been hunting.

"What's going on?"

Travis thought about the bodies they had seen. And he thought about the trail they had crossed. A small party of horsemen. White men because the horses had worn shoes. The few clear marks he'd seen had showed him that. The trail wasn't more than a day or two old.

Finally he turned toward her. "I don't like this. I think maybe we'd better head back to El Paso."

"Why?"

"There are too many people out here. Too much going on all of the sudden."

"Someone else will get to the gold," she said.

"No. Not now. Besides, according to the diary, it's been sitting there for almost two hundred years and no one has found it yet."

"No one has been looking for it," she said. "Or rather, there weren't the people around here to look for it. Now there are, and if we don't get to it, we're going to lose it."

There was a sudden burst of firing. A wild thirty seconds that echoed among the hills. It faded slowly. Travis looked off to the west, toward the mountains there.

"Sounds like someone's gotten into real trouble," he said. He kept scanning the horizon, looking for a sign of the ambush or the fighting but could see nothing.

"I want to push on," said Crockett. "My father would have wanted it that way."

"He wouldn't have wanted for you to get killed."

"You don't know that the shooting will affect us," she said.

"No," said Travis, agreeing. "But there is too much going on out here."

Then, to the north of them, three riders appeared. They were not much more than specks with tiny clouds of dust swirling above and behind them. At first they had no apparent destination, but then spotted the wagon and turned toward it. They increased their pace, galloping down at Travis and Crockett.

Travis wrapped the reins around the brake handle and lifted his Winchester from the back. He cocked it once and let the hammer down with his thumb.

"Who're they?'" asked Crockett.

Travis didn't know, so he didn't answer. He didn't like the idea of three men riding down on him like that. As they came closer, he realized that they were anything but friendly.

"Out of the wagon," he said.

"What?"

"Get out of the wagon and get down." He leaped to the ground and dropped to one knee. He raised his rifle and aimed but hesitated. He didn't want to start an Indian war by picking off a couple of braves who only appeared unfriendly.

And then he thought about the bodies near the watering hole and knew that the Apaches were not coming at him to discuss it. They were going to kill and loot. He aimed at the lead rider, fired, worked the lever, fired, and got into a rhythm.

The first Indian seemed to live a charmed life. Travis fired at him a dozen times, but he didn't react. He rode on, suddenly screaming. And then he sat upright and raised his hands almost as if to surrender. Slowly he fell back over the rear of his horse.

Travis had now emptied his rifle. He tossed it up over the side of the wagon and drew his revolver. The Apaches were shooting back. Spaced shots that were wild. Nothing came close to them.

Crockett stood for a moment, reached into the box of the wagon, and dragged out the shotgun she had brought. She disappeared a moment later.

One of his horses suddenly screamed in pain. It reared back, hampered by the leather harness holding it to the tongue of the wagon. It fell to its knees and then collapsed, blood pumping from its chest. The other horse tried to rear and then tried to run, but the brake of the wagon and the body of the other animal held it in place.

Travis squeezed off four shots rapidly, but missed. One brave held his rifle over his head, screaming his rage. Travis knew that the wagon was now stuck. With a horse dead, there was no way for them to run for it.

Both the Apaches closed on them. Travis climbed to his feet, turned his right side toward the Indians, and lowered his right hand slowly. He fired once and the second brave slipped to the ground.

From the right came a twin boom, boom. Crockett was standing there with the shotgun. She fired both barrels as the last of the braves neared her. The force of the buckshot lifted him from the back of the horse and threw him to the ground. He rolled over a couple of times and didn't move.

"You okay?" asked Travis.

She didn't answer, her eyes on the bleeding body of the Apache. She nodded once. Her hands clutched the shotgun tightly, her knuckles white.

Travis glanced at the three bodies and then turned. He snatched his rifle from the rear of the wagon and began shoving rounds into it. When he had it loaded, he chambered a round and then let the hammer down.

He reloaded his pistol and jammed it into his holster and then pulled his knife. He crouched near the body of the horse and began cutting away the leather harness. He flipped the straps out of the way and then realized that one horse would not be able to pull the wagon. At least not pull it far, and he wasn't about to hitch his own horse to the wagon. It had not been trained to pull a load. It wouldn't know how to react.

Crockett still stood with the shotgun in her hands. Her face was white, sweat dripping form her chin. She didn't look very good. In a quiet voice, she asked, "What's going to happen now?"

"We've got to get the hell out of here," he said. "They know where we are." He'd moved around and now was working to free the second horse from the leather. He looked up at her. "Can you ride bareback?"

"Yes."

"We'll have to leave the wagon. No choice there. We try to salvage it and we're going to lose everything."

She moved forward and put the shotgun down carefully, as if it might go off again. She moved to where Travis was standing and then reached up to pat the horse. Her color was improving rapidly.

Travis left her and walked to the rear of the wagon where his horse was tied. He lifted the blanket and then the saddle out of the wagon bed and tossed them onto the animal. He quickly adjusted it and cinched it and then untied the reins.

"We leave everything?" said Crockett.

"Everything. We get out now and ride for El Paso," said Travis.

She tugged at the harness and then swung herself up onto the horse's back. It pranced to the right, lowered its head, and snorted but did nothing to unseat her.

Travis picked up the shotgun, looked at Crockett hanging onto the horse and realized that there was no way for her to carry it. He'd have to leave it in the wagon though he knew that meant the Apaches would get it, not that another weapon would make any difference.

"They're coming," said Crockett suddenly, her voice tight.

Travis looked up. Half a dozen men had appeared, riding down the slope toward them. Travis climbed into the saddle, wheeled his horse around to the south, and spotted another two or three coming at them from that direction.

"Damn!" He didn't know which way to go. The only thing he knew was that the road back to El Paso was blocked. "That way!" he shouted. "To the west."

Crockett wheeled her horse around and dug her heels into it. It was reluctant to gallop. It broke into a half trot, its head held high. But then Crockett seemed to communicate her panic to the animal and it began to run.

Travis let her get going and then fell in behind her. He glanced back but the Apaches were ignoring them. They were all heading right for the wagon. That had bought them a few minutes. Just a few.

Chapter Nineteen
The Deserts of West Texas
August 26, 1863

The position was defensible and that was all that Davis wanted. A place where they could fan out, cover the approaches, and have half a chance of surviving. The rocky overhangs meant that the Apaches couldn't get behind them or above them and shoot down on them. They'd have to come at them from the front, over open ground. With repeating rifles, Davis knew they could hold off a battalion. Until the ammo ran out.

There was no water either, but Davis figured the ammo would run out before they ran out of water. If they could survive until nightfall, they could split up, each man for himself. Some of them were sure to get away then.

"Got Bradford watching the horses," said Bailey. "Webster's on the right, by that big rock, watching for them from that direction."

"Tell Bradford to forget the horses. They'll stay here until the shooting starts and once it does, we're going to need every gun."

"We lose the horses and we won't be able to get out of here."

"I think," said Davis quietly, "that we're going to have to get out on foot after dark anyway."

Before Bailey could respond, one of the men yelled, "I got riders coming at us."

Davis ran forward, and leaned across a hot rock. There were two men riding fast and behind them was a group chasing them. It was obvious what was happening.

"Take out the second group. Fire when you have a good target. Be careful of the men in front."

He hesitated, waiting for the troops to respond with a "Yes sir," and then remembered that these were civilians. They would fire when they wanted, and they would keep shooting until they were out of ammo or had decided that the good targets were gone. No fire discipline.

The two riders in front suddenly veered to the rocks as if they had decided to make a stand. Davis wanted them to know that help was around, but he didn't want to frighten them. If firing broke out suddenly, they might assume it was another bunch of Apaches. He leaped to the top of the rock, made sure that his hat was pulled down, and aimed his rifle at the second group. He fired once, twice, three times.

The lead rider turned and then glanced at him. He turned again, now riding directly toward the rocks. He had decided that help would be found among the rocks.

With that, Davis dropped back to the ground. He leaned over the rock, bracing his elbow and hand against it to steady his aim. He followed one of the riders, trying to lead him, and fired again with no results.

Now the rest of the men with him began to shoot. The two front riders ducked low, riding straight for the rocks. The Apaches followed for a moment and then turned away. One of them was hit and let out a scream. Another fell from his horse and then jumped to his feet, staggering away from the riflemen.

They kept shooting as fast as they could. The Apaches wheeled and fled. The one man on the ground kept moving away from them until he was hit again. He dropped and didn't move.

The horsemen reached the rocks and as they did, they leaped from the saddle. One of them jerked his rifle from the scabbard, whirled and aimed, but then didn't fire. The Apaches were already out of range.

The second man slipped to the ground and stood watching the fleeing Indians. He held the reins in his left hand. When they disappeared and the firing ended, he turned and looked up into the rocks.

Davis came down and held out a hand. "Name's Davis," he said, and then stopped. "You were in the bar."

"Name's Freeman. Yeah, I was in the bar." He studied Davis for a moment and then asked, "You the bartender?"

"Was."

"So you're out here for the same reason. Looking for the gold that old man talked about."

"Yeah," said Davis. "Somebody killed that old man. Knifed him."

"I'd heard," said Freeman.

"Yeah," said Davis again. "Better get your horses back out of the way. The Apaches will be back."

"Guess we're not going to find the gold now," said Freeman. He shot a glance at his partner.

"Not for a while anyway," said Davis.

They reached the top of a ridge and Travis stopped. The Apaches who had been chasing them were still out of sight. They were probably still at the wagon.

He turned and looked down into the next valley. There was a shallow river through it and mountains off to the right. There had been firing from that direction, but it had stopped. He could see nothing of interest below him.

"We head back to El Paso now?" asked Crockett.

"No," said Travis. "We keep heading to the west for a while longer. The Apaches were to the south of us. This should take us away from them."

"Down there," she said.

"Down toward the river. We'll let the horses drink and maybe take a break."

He took another quick look, but the landscape was still bare. He started down the slope, moving slowly, letting the horse rest. He wanted to be ready if they had to make a run for it again.

"You think we can get back to El Paso today?" she asked.

That was a question that he didn't want to answer. He thought that they'd be two or three days getting back to El Paso. They'd have to avoid the direct route because that's where the Apaches would be. Two or three days, but probably no more than that.

He ignored the question. He kept his eyes moving, searching the horizon and the desert around them for the enemy. He didn't want to be surprised again.

And he kept looking at the shallow river with the mountains to the north of it. Just as had been described by Crockett's father.

He noticed that Crockett had spotted it, too. She kept looking back at him and then at the river. Finally she asked, "You think that's it?"

"It's close," he said. "But remember what the diary said. Wagons burned on the bank. And your father mentioned that and bones of the dead."

"We're close," she said. "I know it. I can feel it."

"But we don't have the time to look around," said Travis. "Not with the hostiles running loose."

She turned toward the river. "We're this close. We've got to take a look."

That was an idea that didn't appeal to Travis. Not with Apaches running around shooting at everyone. The smart thing was to get out now. Remember where they had been and come back when the Indian problem had been settled.

They reached the valley floor and moved along the bank of the river. There were trees, small trees, along the bank, just as described in the diary, but the trees that the Spaniard had written about would be huge unless they had been swept away in floods. Which would have also carried away the debris of the burned wagons.

"Can't be here," said Travis. "Can't be."

"Why not?" asked Crockett.

Travis stopped and climbed from the saddle. He stuck a hand into the sand and let it run through his fingers. Nothing. He stood and surveyed the ground. Still nothing.

But the river was shallow, as had been reported in the diary. And there were bluffs opposite, maybe a mile away, and beyond them the mountains.

Travis began walking along the bank, his eyes on the sand. To have found it so quickly, so close to El Paso would mean that others must have found it. And then he realized that no one believed the story. They listened to the prospector spinning his tails of Spanish gold, bought him drinks for the entertainment, and then forgot about it as quickly as possible. They didn't ride out in search of it.

And he had more information than most. He'd seen the diary and the map and knew what to look for. He knew all the clues. Others only knew some of them.

Crockett stayed mounted, following him slowly. She didn't say a word now. She, too, was looking for the remains of the wagons, because it would tell them where to cross the river. It would help pinpoint the cave where the gold had been stored by the Apaches.

After fifteen minutes he spotted something partially buried in the sand.

He stopped, pulled at it, and came up with a charred piece of wood.

"Wagon?" asked Crockett.

"Could be anything," said Travis tossing it away. "Could be anything at all."

They'd suddenly forgotten about the Apaches that were roaming the desert. They forgot about the firing they'd heard or the danger they were in. Gold fever had driven everything from their minds.

Travis was no longer walking in a straight line. He was weaving over the bank of the river, kicking at the sand. He turned up other chunks of burnt wood and then he stopped and stared. In front of him was a line of wood, and laying near it was the charred remains of a wagon wheel. Sticking up so that one end was two or three inches off the ground, was a bone.

"My God!" said Crockett. "This is it."

Travis looked up at her, his head spinning. He stared at the remains of the wagon, at the shallow river, and the bluffs opposite them and knew that she was right. The gold was hidden in a cave no more than a mile from them. They had found it.

He took a step toward the river and then something made him look back the way they'd come. They might have found the path to the gold, but the Apaches had found them. It was time to get the hell out or die.

Chapter Twenty
The Deserts of West Texas
August 26, 1863

Travis swung up into the saddle and turned toward the river. The only avenue for escape was the hills to the north. On the open ground in the other directions, the Apaches would eventually run them down and kill them. The only hope was to get lost in the hills or among the rocks to the north.

"Come on," he said, keeping his voice quiet.

Crockett took a quick look and forced her horse into the river. She splashed across it while Travis hung back, watching the approaching Apaches. When she was halfway to the other side, Travis followed.

They scrambled up on the far bank. The Indians had changed their direction and were coming straight for them. Travis looked for a haven but saw nothing.

"That way," he said and dug his heels into the flanks of the horse.

Together, Travis and Crockett rode along the foot of the bluff, searching for a hiding place or a canyon or an arroyo to get them out of the sight of the Apaches. The only thing they saw were small box canyons that lead back into the bluffs and ended in steep cliffs or narrow passages that didn't lead anywhere or provide any protection.

"They're gaining on us," yelled Crockett.

But they were still on the opposite side of the river. The Apaches were riding along the southern bank, chasing them, but were making no move to cross.

"Hurry it up," said Travis. He hung back, trying to protect the rear. He kept his eyes on the Indians.

Crockett stopped suddenly. "Someone in front of us."

Travis turned his attention. There was a second group of riders, still south of the river, but angling for them. A dozen men. Maybe more. They didn't seem concerned about the Indians now chasing Travis and Crockett, and that could only mean they were Apaches, too.

"That tears it," said Travis.

And then, as he was searching for a place to make the last stand, he saw a man stand up on a rock about fifty yards from them.

"Hey," he yelled. "Over here."

"Go!" shouted Travis. "Go!"

Crockett wheeled her horse and took off toward the rocks. Travis was right behind her now, riding for the safety ahead. The Apaches plunged into the river, heading toward them. They began to whoop and shoot. First into the air and then at the fleeing riders.

A volley burst from the rocks in front of them. Three of the Apaches fell, two into the river and one on the bank. A horse went down, spilling its rider into the water. That was enough to turn the attack for the moment.

Travis caught Crockett as she disappeared behind a rock. As he came around it, she was off the horse and laying on the ground. For an instant he thought that she had been hit. As he leaped from the saddle, forgetting about his horse, he saw her turn and then grin awkwardly.

"Fell off," she said.

Travis knelt beside her. "You okay?"

"I'm fine. Just slipped off as I tried to stop." She looked at the men standing around her.

Travis helped her to her feet, and looked at one of the men. He stared for a moment and said, "I know you, don't I?"

"Name's Davis and I used to tend bar in Sweetwater."

"Right," said Travis.

"You're the closed-mouth man," said Davis.

"What the hell are you doing here?"

Davis shrugged and said, "I could ask you the same thing, but I think that's obvious. We're searching for the gold."

"You believed that story?" asked Travis.

"As you did," said Davis, "otherwise you wouldn't be here now."

"I think they're gathering for another attack," yelled one of the men.

"How many you got here?" asked Travis.

"With you two we're back to fifteen. Lost a couple to the Apaches."

"How long you been here?" asked Travis.

"Most of the morning. Chased in here just as you were." Davis glanced at him and then his animal. "You have much ammo?"

"Fifty, sixty rounds for the rifle and that much for the pistol."

"That's going to be the problem now," said Davis. "We run out of ammo and they're going to climb all over us."

"Here they come," yelled one of the men.

"Come on," said Davis. "We'll need your gun."

Travis looked at Crockett. "You stay here and stay down. I don't want you getting hurt now."

She reached up and grabbed his hand. "Don't let them take me alive."

"Nobody's going to take anyone," said Travis. He started to head up into the rocks and then stopped. He pulled his pistol from the holster. "You'd better hang onto this."

"Thanks," she said. She held his eyes for a moment and nodded to the rear.

Travis knew what she was saying. They were probably closer to that cave now. The entrance to it had to be around there somewhere. She didn't want to say anything in case the men around them didn't know how close it was.

"I know," said Travis. He then followed Davis up into the rocks.

The Apaches were about halfway across the river. There were more of them. All the groups had joined so that there were fifty or sixty braves now.

From the right came a rippling fire. Two or three of the men shooting into the crowd. One brave fell from his horse but then leaped to his feet, standing in the knee-deep water. He ran forward, grabbed the neck of the animal, and climbed back on.

"Open fire!" yelled Davis suddenly. He fired his own weapon once, cocked it, but didn't shoot again.

Travis raised his rifle but didn't fire. He waited until the Apaches had reached the near side of the river and slowed as they tried to gain the bank. Then, with the targets sitting still, he opened fire. His first round missed, but the second shoved a brave from his horse. He fell into the soft sand and rolled down into the water.

There was firing all around him then. The men were up and shooting as fast as they could. One was screaming as he shot. A constant wail of anger as he pumped rounds into the Apaches.

They began to shoot back. Bullets snapped overhead and whined off the rocks. One of the men dropped his rifle and slipped from his position. Blood stained the side of his head. A second tumbled from behind a rock and didn't move.

The Apaches were closer, riding straight at them. Travis fired as fast as he could, working the lever and pulling the trigger in a single, smooth motion. The Indians were howling, waving their weapons, and firing into the air.

Travis emptied his weapon and then slipped down behind the rock. He struggled to work the bullets from the loops in his belt. His fingers felt like sausages. He had trouble controlling them. A task that had once been so simple was suddenly complex. The bullets were too large, jammed into the loops. Pulling them free, he couldn't seem to hit the side to slide the rounds into the weapon.

"There's too many of them," yelled one man.

"Someone help me! I'm hit."

Travis stretched slightly and looked over the top of the rock. The Apaches were closer. They had spread out and some of them were on foot now. They were searching for cover and were firing up into the rocks.

Travis whirled and aimed, but the Apaches were all gone. They had found hiding places. The firing tapered, becoming sporadic. Travis searched for a target and found none. He waited, watching.

And then, suddenly, the scene from Gettysburg flared in his mind. Hundreds of men, thousands of them, running at him. Hundreds of them falling and dying. It was the reason that he had gotten out of Pennsylvania. He'd wanted no part of the slaughter that warfare had become. He didn't want to hide behind rocks or fences and shoot at other men.

But this was different, he told himself. Before, two men with stars on their shoulders had decided that men should fight and die. Here, in Texas, it was a matter of survival. If he didn't stop the Apaches, they would capture him and kill him. At Gettysburg, if he hadn't fired, it would have only been one fewer weapon and the results would have been the same. His survival, and the survival of Emma Crockett, hadn't depended on what he did then.

That made it different. Emma Crockett was depending on him. Stop the Apaches so they could get out. The gold wasn't important at the moment. Getting out was. They could come back in a year or two, but at the moment they had to survive.

A brave stood up and aimed into the rocks. He fired and dropped from sight. Travis aimed at the top of the rock and waited. As the Apache stood again, Travis fired. The Indian lost his rifle and fell back.

The firing tapered, and then the Apaches began to slowly withdraw. They covered one another as they worked their way back to the riverbank.

Davis slipped down to where Travis was crouched. "I think we'll have an hour or so."

"We're going through the ammo pretty fast."

"I know. And when it runs out . . ."

"Maybe we should try to get out now."

"I figured we'd have a better chance after dark. Some of us could make it then." He studied Travis for a moment and then asked, "You have military service?"

"Some."

"Rest of these guys don't. We've got to get them organized. Teach them some discipline."

Travis shook his head. "You're not going to be able to do it in an hour."

Davis was about to protest and then nodded. He pushed himself up and said, "I'm going to check on the others."

Travis slipped from his position and made his way down to where Crockett knelt, the pistol held in her right hand. Her eyes were closed.

"Emma," he said.

She looked up at him. "What?"

"They've pulled back. For the moment."

She glanced around as if looking for conspirators. Lowering her voice, she asked, "Do you know where we are? Exactly where we are?"

"Yes."

"The cave has to be around here somewhere. Up in the rocks a little higher," She said.

"Not much we can do about it now."

"I want to go look for it."

"No," said Travis. Then, realizing she wouldn't accept that, he added, "Too many eyes around to see that, not to mention the Apaches. They're going to be working their way through the rocks to get at us."

"But the gold," she said. "We're so close to it. I've got to find it."

"Not now," said Travis. "Later."

"How much later?" she asked. And then, "You think we're going to get out of this?"

"I think we've got a good chance if the men don't waste their ammo. That's going to be the key."

"Then this might be my only chance to see the gold."

Travis knelt then so that he was no longer looking down at her. "We'll be able to come back later. A year or two."

"Or five or ten," she said. "You don't know how tough the Apaches can be."

"They're stirred up now," said Travis. "Next year they might all be happy on the reservation."

"Would you be?" she asked

"I don't know. All I'm saying is that next year things might be tamer and we won't have to worry about the Apaches. Right now it's too dangerous."

"I want to see the gold," she said. "I have to see it."

"Let's get out of this first and then we can worry about the gold."

"If we get out of this," she reminded him.

Travis shrugged and then agreed with her. "If we get out of this. Right now I've got to get back up there and watch for the Indians. You going to be okay here?"

"I'll be fine," she said.

Travis stood and then hesitated. "Don't do anything foolish," he warned her.

"I won't."

Chapter Twenty-One
The Deserts of West Texas
August 26, 1863

Emma Crockett waited until Travis was out of sight and then got to her feet. All the men were at the edge of the bluffs, hidden in the rocks, watching for the Apaches. No one was watching her. No one cared about her for the moment.

During the fight, after the first few frightening minutes were over and she knew that the Apaches would not get at them then, she had studied the ground behind them. There were paths in the rocks. There were overhangs that wrapped the ground in shadows. There were a dozen places that could have concealed the entrance to the cave. There were paths through rocks leading higher, some of them probably up to the top of the overhang.

She stood there for a moment and tried to remember the point where they had ridden across the river. She thought that she could see that point and by drawing a line from there and from the wreckage of the Spanish wagon train, she saw two, maybe three points that could be caves.

She followed one of the paths to the rear, moving quietly and carefully. She noticed two men crouched, watching the river, and she saw the body of one man, his blood staining the sand near him.

She pressed on past them, and into a narrow crack in a huge stone. She stopped there and turned again. From that position she could see down to the river easily. To the west were the bodies of the Indians killed that morning. To the east was the place where she and Travis had found the burned wagons.

She slipped through, turning sideways for twenty feet. At one point she had to climb up on the side and push herself along the sun-hot stone. She dropped to the ground and walked along. In front of her was a large opening in the rock. There was a mesa in front of it that dropped off sharply. From everything she had read in the diary and from the map she had seen, that had to be the entrance to the cave.

The thing she couldn't believe was how easy it was to find. No tiny hole in the rocks that opened into something larger. No disguised entrance that was nearly impossible to find. Standing on the bank of the river, had she had the chance, she might have been able to see the entrance. Of course, without the map and the diary, she wouldn't have known the significance of the cave.

She pushed herself out of the narrow passage and then crouched. She knelt there, studying the cave. She didn't want to rush right to it. She wanted a chance to savor the moment of discovery.

And then she stood and walked forward. At the entrance she stopped. The sunlight didn't penetrate very far. She could see that the floor of the cave dropped away. Sand had spilled from the mesa down into the cave.

She took a step forward and slipped, falling on her behind. She laughed out loud and then clapped a hand over her mouth. The sound seemed to echo through the cave.

She stood again and worked her way deeper into the cave. The entrance narrowed down rapidly so that from the mesa it would look like it was nothing more than an overhang without a cave. But there at the base of it was an opening only six feet high and three or four wide.

Using the rocks, she walked down to the bottom of the opening and peered into the darkness. Inside the cave proper, she could see nothing. There was a coolness blowing up at her that held a musty odor. From deep inside the cave she though she could hear water dripping.

Glancing back at the mesa, she saw that she was still alone. No sounds from anywhere. The Apaches were still making their plans, and those who'd been fighting the Indians were waiting for the next attack.

She kept her back against the rock and slipped around into the cave. There was enough light bleeding in that she could see the stalactites hanging down. The floor was solid rock and tilted down at a forty-five degree angle, but the stone was dry and the footing solid.

She moved down until the floor leveled out. She turned, looking back at the entrance, which was brightly marked by the sunlight. Now, looking back, she saw something that had been invisible before. She climbed back up to it and pulled an old helmet from the sand.

"Spanish?" she asked and then shrugged. She'd seen pictures of the conquistadors all wearing narrow helmets with upsweeping curves that came to a point in the front and rear. The helmet she held looked just like those pictures and was very old and rusting.

She nodded then and felt the excitement pulse through her. A Spanish helmet at the entrance to the cave. Hidden deeper in it would be more treasures. Hidden in it would be the gold that her father had sought most of his life. She had found it so easily. But then, she'd had the clues her father had provided as he tried to identify the river and the mountains. Without knowing where to look, it would have been impossible.

For a moment she stood there looking at the helmet and then she put it down, carefully. She didn't want anything to happen to it. Satisfied that she'd found the cave, she started to work her way out of it. She climbed back to the entrance then stopped.

She realized that the gold was there. Hidden deeper, and that was the whole point. Find the gold. See it and touch it and hold it. Now she was leaving before she did that. She started to turn around to go back but then stopped again. There was no way for her to find the treasure without a torch and some help. She'd have to get Travis.

She scrambled out of the cave and moved back to the mesa. As she crossed it, she saw the Indians were beginning to move again. They were still far off, across the river, but they were beginning the next attack.

Freeman stayed at the far end of the line, aware of Travis. He recognized him and the woman the minute they crossed the river. No question about it. He'd slapped Crosby on the arm and pointed them out, telling him who it was in case he didn't recognize them himself.

Now that the attack had been beaten off, Freeman had slipped down behind a rock where it would be difficult to see him from anywhere. The Apaches wouldn't see him and those with him wouldn't see him.

"What are we going to do?" asked Crosby. "He saw us kill that man."

"I know," said Freeman. "We're going to have to kill him before he tells anyone."

"What about the girl?"

Freeman shrugged. "If he's told her, we'll have to kill her, too. Right now, I don't know."

"We should kill her just to be safe," said Crosby.

Freeman laughed. "Funny that we're all searching for the gold and we all end up right here. A shallow river and high bluffs."

"I didn't see any sign of burned wagons," said Crosby.

"We didn't have time to look," said Freeman. "I'll bet if we rode along the bank far enough, we'd find them. We're very close to the gold."

Crosby took off his hat and wiped the sweatband with his finger. He flipped the sweat away. "Everybody's going to know that."

"Not everybody knows who that woman is," said Freeman. "We're sitting pretty right now. That guy doesn't know that we're here. Advantages are all ours."

"Except for the Apaches," said Crosby.

Freeman turned and stood. He glanced out at the river and then the open ground leading to the bluff. He saw no movement out there. Satisfied that the Indians were not sneaking toward them, he slipped down again.

"They're going to hit us again," said Freeman. "Everyone knows that Maybe when they do we should see it we can't kill that man. With all the lead flying around, no one's going to know how anyone got hit."

"I'd feel better if he was dead," said Crosby.

"Then here's what we do. When the Apaches come at us, we slip along the line. We find him and the first chance we get, we put a bullet into him. When that's done, we turn our attention to the Apaches."

"Who does it?"

"Whoever gets the chance. We kill him just as soon as we can."

Crosby pulled his revolver from the holster and checked it carefully. He knew that it was fully loaded. That had been the first thing he'd done after the Apaches retreated, but now, with the murder plan in front of him, he checked it again. It was something to do.

Freeman heard someone coming and pulled his pistol just in case, but it wasn't the right man. It was one of those who had been there from the beginning. Freeman lowered the hammer carefully.

"Davis wants to know how much ammo you've got."

"Why?"

"'Cause he doesn't want any one person runnin' out when them Apaches attack. Wants everyone to have enough. Wants to make sure everyone has enough."

"Got enough," said Freeman.

"'Kay. You stay here and cover the flank. You get into trouble, you sing out."

As the man disappeared, Crosby asked, "What'd he mean cover the flank."

"The side. We stay on this side so that the Apaches can't hit it suddenly."

"But we're not going to be here," said Crosby.

"Doesn't matter," said Freeman. "Apaches are going to come right at us from the front anyway."

Crosby turned so that he could look down toward the river. He noticed movement there, focused on it, and then said, "Here they come."

Chapter Twenty-Two
The Deserts of West Texas
August 26, 1863

"Here they come again!" yelled one of the men as he began to shoot.

Travis thumbed back the hammer on his rifle and then waited as the Apaches leaped from the far bank and began the charge across the shallow river. They were three or four hundred yards away. Inside the range of his rifle, which meant he could hit the target if it held still long enough. He'd wait for them to get closer.

The attacking Indians were whooping and yelling, but they had yet to fire a round. They knew they could hit nothing from horseback, and they didn't want to waste their ammo. He took that as a good sign.

They reached the near bank and began to fight their way up it. As the horses hesitated there, trying to find solid footing, Travis aimed and fired. A horse fell to its side, spilling the rider into the river. As he stood up, Travis fired again, knocking him down.

The firing from the rocks became a steady rattle. No longer were the men firing with wild abandon. They were picking their targets now, not just blazing away.

The Apaches made it up out of the river and were riding across open ground. Travis fired again and again but missed. He saw one huge Indian holding a rifle high and aimed at his chest. The man, seeming to be uninjured, leaped from the back of his pony, took two running steps, and dropped to the sand. He lost his grip on his rifle.

There didn't seem to be as many of them this time as there had been in the past. But they leaped from the backs of their ponies and ran to the cover of the scattered rocks. Once there, they began firing up at the white men.

Travis threw a couple of rounds down, just to let them know that he was still alive, but then held his fire. There were no huge ammo wagons hidden behind him. There wasn't a battalion of supply people ready to run ammo to him when he ran low. What he had was all that he had, and he had to conserve it. But not in a way that told the Apaches that.

He laid down, looked around the bottom of the rocks, and watched smoke from the firing of the Apaches roll up at them. He listened to the sounds of it. A few weapons firing slowly. He slipped back and pushed himself along the ground, out of sight of the enemy. He reached a second rock and moved up so that he was kneeling behind it.

He took a moment and shoved several rounds into the side of his rifle, making sure that it was fully loaded. He then popped up and looked down. Three Apaches were working their way through the rocks, trying to sneak up on the side while those out in front, between them and the river, held everyone's attention.

Travis aimed at the closest, fired, swung at the second, and fired as the sights touched him. As the last of the Apaches tried to dive for cover, Travis fired the last time. The Indian collapsed to the dirt and didn't move.

Now he took time to check the other two. Both were still down and he could see a spreading stain of blood from the first he'd shot. There was no sign that the second man had been hit. Travis aimed at a point near the center of the man's back and put a round there.

There was a sound behind him, but Travis thought nothing of it. That had to be one of the men with them. Davis had sent someone to make sure that the Apaches didn't out flank them.

The round snapped by him and whined off the rock. Splinters from it and from the bullet struck the side of his face. Travis, without thinking about it, dived to the right and rolled. He worked the lever of his rifle and fired as soon as he saw the target.

The round took the man in the center of the chest. Travis was sure that he could hear the snap of bone as the bullet smashed the sternum. The man grunted in surprise and dropped the pistol he held in his right hand. He fell back on his butt and rolled over.

Travis stared at him, sure that his quick reactions had cost a friend his life. He leaped to his feet and moved toward the down man, first feeling for a pulse, and then rolling him over. He stared into the face of the dead man and recognized him instantly. He'd been one of the men from Kansas who had killed the old prospector.

"That's right," said a voice.

Travis looked and saw the other man standing there, grinning at him. "Thought your quick finger had killed a friend, didn't you?" he said.

Travis nodded. He knew that there was no way he could swing the barrel of his rifle around to shoot the second Kansan. He needed to cock it first. If he made any move like that the man would kill him immediately.

"I have just one question. Does the woman know who I am?"

"No," he said simply.

"We're in the right place then?"

Travis shook his head. "I don't know about that. We were running from the Apaches."

"You don't lie very well. And even if that isn't the right river, or the right place on the river, we're damned close to being there."

Travis didn't respond. He was measuring the angles, wondering if he could throw sand at the man, if he could somehow jump him, or if he could somehow get his weapon turned on him with a round chambered before the man cut him in two.

"You should have just worried about bedding the orphaned daughter," said the man. "You shouldn't have come out here."

Firing erupted near them. There was a whoop from an Apache and the man glanced in that direction. Travis reacted immediately, jerking at the lever of his rifle, but before he could get the round chambered or the barrel of the weapon pointed at the man, it was too late. The man's pistol was pointed right at his face, and he was grinning broadly.

"I'm not that stupid," he said.

Suddenly, a third eye appeared in his forehead, just above and to the right of his nose. There was a crack of bone and a sudden spurt of blood. The man fell back, firing once into the air, dead before he hit the ground.

Travis whirled, now with a round chambered. He saw Crockett standing there with the pistol in her hand. She was still aiming it at the dead man, but this time her face wasn't pale or her knuckles white.

"He killed my father, didn't he?" she asked. Her face was a mask of fury as she stared at the body.

"Yes," said Travis.

"You knew they were here and you didn't tell me."

"No, I didn't know until they tried to kill me."

"Were they the ones you saw in El Paso?"

Travis was aware of the Apaches below them. There was sporadic firing from the rocks. The force of the attack seemed to be at the front of the position, away from them.

"Were they the ones you saw in El Paso?" Her voice was now hard, strained.

He swiped at the sweat on his face and rubbed his lips with the back of his hand. It was suddenly time to tell the truth. Time to be honest. "Yeah," he said, nodding. "They were."

"And you were going to let them go scot-free." She spat the accusation at him.

"No. It wasn't the right time then. I didn't know if they had friends in El Paso."

"Bull," she said.

Travis wanted to say something to her about it. Wanted her to understand that it hadn't been the right time to deal with them in El Paso. He had known where to look for them, knew enough about them to find them later, but he couldn't explain all that to her.

"You knew and you didn't say a word to me."

"It wasn't the right time."

"Would it have ever been the right time? Ever?"

Shooting tapered and then flared. Travis turned and leaned against the rock. He saw two Apaches running across the open ground and he fired down at one of them. He saw the sand erupt behind the man and then watched as he disappeared among the light trees at the side of the river.

Travis wiped his face on the back of his hand and searched for signs of the Apaches. The sound of firing was tapering around him. He'd been unaware of the battle as he'd stared into the weapon held by the man from Kansas. Everything had faded into the background as he waited for the man to shoot him.

Crockett joined him, crouching next to him. She was still pale but seemed to have forgotten about the dead man behind them. "What's happening down there?" she asked. Her voice was quieter. The anger fading.

"Apaches are falling back to the river now," he said quietly.

"They'll try again?"

"I'm sure they will. They're chipping away at us and between you and me, we've killed two of our own."

"I had to shoot him," she said. Her voice was quiet.

"Oh," said Travis, "that wasn't a criticism. You saved my life. He was going to kill me."

"I heard you tell him that I didn't know who he was, but I didn't think he'd really shoot you. Was he the one who killed my father?"

"Yeah. Stabbed him once in the chest. I couldn't stop him."

"Would you have told me?"

"Yeah," said Travis. "The time wasn't right in El Paso. Once we were out of there and had some time, I would have said something."

She dropped to the ground and lifted her hand to her face. She wiped away the sweat. "You should have told me in El Paso."

"Yeah," he said. "I should have." Travis was suddenly uncomfortable with the conversation. Changing the subject, he said, "We're going to have to get out of here. I don't think we can repulse another attack."

She ignored that. She turned to face him. Sweat was beaded on her forehead and upper lip. Her color was bad and she looked as if she was about to be sick, but instead announced, "I found it."

For a moment Travis didn't understand what she meant because she'd shifted subjects so fast.

"The gold is here," she said. "I found the cave and I went inside."

"You saw the gold?"

"No," she admitted. "But I found an old Spanish helmet in the entrance. The gold is in there somewhere."

Travis turned to look at her. Her hair was coming loose and there was dirt smeared on her face but that wasn't surprising, considering. He glanced back at the ground below them littered with the bodies of the dead.

That gold had brought them out there. The gold was responsible for the deaths of the people around them. For the two that he and Crockett had killed, those shot by the Apaches, and the Indians who had died. A lot of people dead because of the Spanish gold. And that didn't even include Crockett's father, murdered because he told the story about it.

The one thing that he was going to regret was that he hadn't gotten to see the gold. It was close to them now. Crockett had gotten close to it.

"I want to see it," he said suddenly.

"I can take you there," said Crockett. "We can see it." She had forgotten about the dead men. She had forgotten about the two men who had killed her father. She had forgotten everything except the gold.

Travis thought about that and realized that there was nothing more that he could do there. The Apaches would either attack again or they wouldn't. If they did, they'd probably kill everyone in the rocks.

"Let's do it," said Travis. "Let's do it while we have the chance."

She glanced at the bodies of the two dead men. Flies were already beginning to gather, their buzzing cutting through the hot, desert air. Their bodies were beginning to stink. The ground under them was wet with their blood, the odor of hot copper around them.

She pointed the pistol at the one she'd killed. "I just can't get upset over that. Now knowing that he killed my father. He deserved to die."

"No reason to be upset," said Travis, quietly. "He's the one who stabbed your father. No reason he had to do it, he just did, probably afraid that your father would tell me the secret of the gold."

"Then I'm glad I killed him."

"So am I," said Travis.

"But you should have told me in El Paso."

He nodded again. "I should have."

Chapter Twenty-Three
The Deserts of West Texas
August 26, 1863

Travis wasn't sure what to do. He knew that two more of the defenders were dead, but didn't know if others had been killed. He didn't know how much ammo was left or how strong the Apaches were. Davis's plan, to hold out until dark and then slip away, might have been ruined during the last attack.

So, he followed Crockett as she made her way behind what would have been the front line if they had been a military unit and had a front line. They kept down, using the cover that the rocks provided, and slipped away to the east.

"Through here," she said. Standing, she pointed. "That's where we crossed the river and where we found the wagons. Just like it said in the diary."

"Sure," he said.

"This passage leads to the entrance to the cave. If we'd come straight up from the river, we'd have only had to climb a small hill and cross the mesa."

"Lead on," said Travis.

She entered the passage, bracing herself on the rocks and lifting her feet to swing them forward. There were points where it was nearly impossible to get through, but once they did, Travis saw the cave's entrance.

"You can see this from the riverbank."

"Yeah, but you have to get into it and climb down to find the cave proper."

"Show me," he said.

She looked at him and then moved down to the entrance of the cave. "Just through here is where I found that helmet. Right inside."

"But you didn't see the gold."

"No."

"Maybe it's not there," he said, but knew it would be. Everything that her father had said and everything that had been written in the diary was there, from the wagons burned after the ambush to the Apaches roaming around guarding the ground. If everything else was true, then there was no reason to believe that the story of the gold was false. It would be there if they got deep enough into the cave.

"Come on," she said. She moved along the wall of the opening, just as she had done before. They reached the real entrance to the cave.

"Feel the cool air?" she asked.

"Yeah."

They entered the cave and then stopped. Crockett crouched and pointed to the helmet. "Spanish?"

"I think so."

"This is all the farther I got," she said. "I wouldn't have been able to see the gold."

"There must be something around here," said Travis. "If the gold is deeper in the cave, then there must be a way of lighting the path."

"I didn't see anything."

Travis moved farther down to where the floor leveled. He could see the outline of the passageway that lead back into the mountain. The air there was cooler and mustier. He reached the point where the front chamber ended. There looked to be a smudge at the top, like that made from a torch. To one side was a long stick. Travis bent and picked it up and found that the top had been wrapped in cloth.

"Here," he said. "Found a torch."

"Light it," she said.

"This isn't going to last very long," he said. "Fifteen or twenty minutes at the most."

"Light it," she said. The excitement was unmistakable in her voice.

Travis did as ordered and then ducked, pushing it out in front of him. He could see through the narrow passage that was only a few feet long.

There was a blackness behind that. He stepped in and found that it was even cooler. The air caught the flame of the torch and made it flicker.

Travis slipped along the passage. Crockett was right behind him. He noticed that the rock was smooth, as if someone had carved the passage from the stone, creating an artificial tunnel. At the other end, it opened up into another huge chamber so large that he couldn't see either the ceiling above him or the far side of it. The light front he torch just wasn't bright enough.

Crockett moved out of the passage to stand beside him. "I don't see anything."

Travis took a step forward and then another. It looked as if there was a dirty brick wall cutting the chamber in half. The wall was about five feet high and thirty or forty feet long.

"What's that?" asked Crockett.

Travis wasn't sure. He walked toward it and bent close. He reached down and felt the cool smoothness of metal. He turned to face her and said, "It's the gold."

"What?"

Travis handed her the torch and pulled one of the bars from the stack. He realized the wall was three feet thick. There was a hell of a lot of gold there.

Holding the bar up, he pulled his knife and scraped at the dull gray surface. It flaked away, revealing the bright, shiny gold underneath it.

"The gold," he said.

"All of that?" she asked, pointing at the wall.

"All of that. Every single brick of it is gold. More than you and I could ever need. More than all of us here could ever need."

"Good God," she said.

Travis knew exactly what she meant. His knees were weak, his stomach filled with butterflies, and his head was spinning. There was more gold there than he could imagine in one place. More gold than he thought existed anywhere in the world. There was enough for him to buy most of the United States and a good chunk of Mexico.

"Good God doesn't cover it," he said.

"I had no idea. I figured a chest or two filled with coins. Maybe some precious stones. I didn't know there would be a wall of gold."

Travis slipped along it, touching it, making sure that someone hadn't substituted a few clay bricks to even things out. Everywhere he touched, it was obviously metal. He came to the end of the wall and looked behind it, but it was too dark to see anything.

"Hold the torch up."

There were two skeletons visible, both wearing rusting armor. The helmet on the skull of one was partially crushed, telling Travis what had killed him. The hands of the other skeleton were missing and the right leg was broken.

Crockett moved around toward him and then stopped suddenly. "Spanish?"

"I think so. Maybe wounded in the fight and brought here as some kind of sacrifice."

Travis noticed that the breeze had picked up and that the air was colder now. It was blowing up from somewhere deeper in the mountain.

There was nothing else behind the wall of gold. The chamber tapered again, but there were two exits from the great room. The floor of it was uneven and there were a couple of stalagmites there. From somewhere came the sound of dripping water.

Travis stood staring at the wall for a few moments more and then said, "We'd better get out of here."

"With nothing?"

"Emma, we take anything out with us and that's going to tell the others we found the treasure."

"So we share it with them. There's more than enough for everyone."

"But I don't trust those men. Some might think that not sharing it will leave that much more for them. They won't realize that you can't live in more than one house at at time, or ride more than one horse. They'll want it all."

"You don't know that."

"No, but I'm not going to put it to the test until I learn more about them."

"Then what are we going to do?"

"We'll return to the surface and see what plan Davis has for getting us all out of here."

She tugged at one of the bars and realized how heavy it was. Not something to be carried around in the pocket. "I guess we'll leave it."

"For now," said Travis. He reached out and touched the wall again. "But we know right where it is and we can come back later for it. Some of it."

The torch was burning down and the light was fading. Crockett began to move toward the corridor that would take them out of the chamber. She stopped short and turned, but there was not evidence of the wall now. It was as if it had disappeared into the darkness.

"It's well hidden," she said. "You almost have to fall over it."

Now she lead the way back through the passage and into the first chamber. They could see the square of light that marked the entrance to the cave.

Travis came out behind her and stopped in his tracks. He looked past her, up at the entrance. From outside he heard the unmistakable sound of gunfire."

"They're attacking again," he said.

"Yeah."

"We'd better get back to help," said Travis.

"We're safe here," she said.

"You stay. They're going to need my gun or the Apaches are going to kill them."

She nodded but didn't say a word.

Travis scrambled up toward the entrance to the cave. When he reached it, he realized that she was right behind him. From outside he heard the sound of the Apaches whooping as the firing tapered to sporadic shots. It didn't sound as if Davis had been able to repulse the last attack.

Chapter Twenty-Four
The Deserts In West Texas
August 26, 1863

The second attack had nearly done them in. Davis had slipped along the line and found that a number of his men had been killed or wounded. Those who had ridden in later were either dead or missing. Bailey had been killed, a bullet through the neck, and Webster was down with a bullet in the knee and a second in the shoulder. Bradford had been hit, too, but not badly. He was more angry than hurt.

Davis checked the ammo, picking up that from the dead and passing it out to the living. It didn't make much of a difference. He didn't tell any of the survivors that it didn't look as if they'd make it to the night so they could slip away. He didn't tell them that the next attack would probably be the last.

He drew the men into a tight ring around him with the wounded in the center of it. If he and the healthy men couldn't fight off the Apaches, it would make no difference to the wounded. Davis had decided that no one would be taken alive. He would take care of the wounded at his last act.

Now there was nothing more he could do. He had a fully-loaded rifle in his hands, a second one propped against the rock, and two pistols jammed into his belt. He sat down, his back to the rock, looked up at the sun, and knew that it wouldn't set for another five or six hours. Much too long.

He pulled the cork from his canteen, took a drink, and sloshed the water around his mouth before swallowing. He took his hat off and wiped the sweat from his forehead.

"When do you think they'll come?" asked Bradford.

"When they get ready and not before. They'll just decide it's time and come at us."

Bradford crouched down. His hands were shaking and his face was pale. Sweat was beaded on his upper lip and he was blinking rapidly. "We're not going to make it, are we?"

Davis thought about answering that question. When the Apaches attacked, he'd need every gun and every man if they were to have any kind of hope. He could lie and maybe lose Bradford when the attack came, or he could tell the truth and maybe lose him now. The truth won.

"I think that we might be able to repulse one more attack, but after that it'll be all over. There are too many of them."

Bradford nodded slowly. "Maybe we should try to get out now."

"I thought about that," said Davis, "but I don't like the odds. In the daylight they'd run us down and kill us one at a time. Here we'll take some of them with us."

"Maybe if we get out, they'll let us go," said Bradford. "Maybe they're mad because we're close to the gold."

"This has nothing to do with the gold," said Davis. "We're in their territory and they're defending it. They won't let us walk out. Especially after what we did at the watering hole."

Bradford closed his eyes for a moment. Sweat dripped down the side of his face and from his chin. It looked as if he was going to pass out and then suddenly, the color came back to his face.

"Okay," he said, nodding. "We'll take the sons o' bitches with us."

Davis didn't say anything to him. He just stood up and turned so that he could watch the river bank. That's where the Apaches were hidden.

They didn't have long to wait. Within minutes the Apaches were on the move again, but this time they weren't attacking across the river on horseback. They were coming up from the near bank, using it and the trees and bushes along it as cover. They were crawling along, from bush to tree to depression, showing as little of themselves as they possibly could. There was no firing from them.

Davis leaned across the sun-hot rock, his rifle tucked into his shoulder. He was looking over the barrel, searching for a target. But the Apaches, having seen that a straight frontal assault might succeed eventually but only at a great loss of life, had decided to sneak forward. They were not going to play the ritualistic game of counting coup as their brothers of the plains did. They were out to kill.

Davis finally began to use the sights. He followed the progress of one brave, and the instant the man was in the sights, he fired. The round hit a stone and whined off into the distance. But that started it. The men with him opened up, their rifles rattling. The Apaches did not shoot back. They dodged from tree to rock to bush, showing themselves briefly and then diving to hide. Bullets slammed into the trees, or kicked up sand, or chipped the rocks. And still the Apaches came on.

Davis caught one of the Indians as he made a final run for the foot of the bluff. The round spun him around, and he threw his rifle into the air. He fell to the sand and didn't move again.

"One down," said Davis quietly, as if speaking to himself.

"Got another coming up here," said Bradford. He fired then, and there was a scream of pain.

But all the Apaches had reached the foot of the bluff near the body of the man just killed, and were not climbing up the rocks. They used the crevices and outcroppings and the depressions to hide. They began to shoot, too. Single shots that chipped at the stones near Davis and his tiny band of defenders.

"Got one to the right," said a voice. "Coming up now."

Davis saw movement out of the corner of his eye, whirled, and fired. The round missed, striking a stone with a high-pitched sound. The Apache leaped in among them, raising a knife over his head. He swung it at Davis who dodged right and fired again. The Apache was hit low, in the stomach. He grabbed at himself and fell, his blood pumping onto the sand.

That marked a change in the battle. While they had been watching the Indians playing the game in front of them, others had been approaching from the sides. A second Indian, and then a third, came over the rocks, leaping among the defenders.

Webster was the first to die. He didn't see the Apache dive over a rock and come at him. The Indian plunged the knife into Webster's back and then shoved him down. He jumped on Webster's back, jerked at his hair and cut his throat.

Davis shot the Apache but it did Webster no good. His blood pumped out onto the sand at the base of a rock. There was an odor of bowel and hot copper. The whole area was beginning to stink of that and gunpowder and sweat.

Bailey died next as one of the Apaches shot him in the face. Bailey might not have realized what was happening. He'd been delirious from the heat and from the pain of his wounds.

Davis watched the others go down one by one. They were shot or stabbed or clubbed. They fought as long as they could, some of them wounded. Finally there was only Davis left alive. The others were lying on the ground around him in bloody heaps. It was apparent that the Apaches planned on taking him alive.

For a moment, they had a stand-off. He was surrounded by the Apaches, who didn't move only because he held a pistol in his hand. He moved it from the chest of one brave to that of another as they would move.

Davis knew that there was no hope now. He was as good as dead. The question was did he want to go easy or hard. He knew the Apaches would keep him alive as long as possible, as they thought of ways to amuse themselves while they tortured him to death.

Grinning suddenly, he turned his pistol on himself, the barrel against his temple. He hesitated briefly, not giving himself time to think. He pulled the trigger.

There was a blinding flash of white light and a deafening roar as pain flared red-hot in his head. The sunlight was fading. Everything was getting dark around him. The sounds were fading, too. Davis had no idea what was happening to him. All he knew was that he must have drunk everything in the bar because he had the granddaddy of all hangovers.

And then he knew nothing at all.

Chapter Twenty-Five
The Deserts of West Texas
August 26, 1863

The firing had tapered to almost nothing when Travis reached the narrow passage that would lead out of the cave. He crouched in the entrance, suddenly unsure of what to do. He could hear the Apaches whooping and screaming, but there was no firing now. He wondered if Davis and the others had been killed.

Crockett approached, leaned close, and whispered, "What's going on?"

"I don't know." Travis stood up but could see nothing. "Maybe you'd better wait here and I'll go take a quick look around."

"I don't want to stay here."

"It's the safest place around right now. I'll be back in a matter of minutes."

She stared at him and finally nodded once. "But you hurry. I'm not going to wait long."

Travis nodded and left the corridor. He kept his back to the solid rock and worked his way up to the mesa in front of the cave. From there he could see nothing. No sign that the Apaches had attacked and none that any of the others were alive. All he could hear was the shouting of the Indians.

Keeping low, he worked his way through the passage, but before he reached the end of it, he saw two Apaches facing away from him. One of them held what looked like the severed arm of a man. The other Indian held a rifle that looked like the one Davis had been using. If that was true, it would mean that Davis was dead.

Without any firing, the only conclusion was that everyone had been killed. He started to slip back into the narrow passage so that he could return to the cave. The noise of the leather of his boots scraping on the stone sounded like the roar of a wounded mountain lion now that he could see the enemy near.

One of the Apaches turned and looked right at him. For an instant the Indian didn't react and then shouted a warning.

Travis whirled and pushed his way back through the passage. He heard the Apaches howling behind him but didn't turn to look at them. He didn't want to waste the time.

He reached the overhang and slipped down into it. Then he turned, saw one Apache in the entrance of it. Travis raised his rifle and fired. The Indian collapsed, falling down so that his body was wedged in it.

Travis scrambled back down to the entrance of the cave. He saw Crockett crouched there, watching him.

"What happened?" she asked.

Travis pushed his way in. "They're all dead."

"You sure?"

"Sure enough and now they're coming after us."

"What are we going to do?"

Travis turned, but the Apaches had not crossed the mesa yet. They were probably still celebrating the deaths of the others. In a few minutes they'd begin moving after him and Crockett. They'd want a clean sweep.

"Back into the cave," he said.

"We'll be trapped in there," she said.

"But they'll only be able to come through one at a time. They won't be able to get at us."

"But we can't get out."

"Right now," said Travis, "I don't see that as a problem. Right now all we can worry about is keeping them away from us."

Crockett moved to the rear, through the passage again. As she did, there was a single shot. The bullet ricocheted down the passageway. The sound echoed through the chambers of the cave, sounding like a battle had started.

Travis followed her and then ran across the first chamber until he was close to the entrance of the second. Opposite him was the bright square that led to the outside.

There was more firing from outside. The bullets whined through the entrance and then bounced around the inside of the chamber.

"Get down," said Travis. "And stay down."

He found a place behind a stalagmite. He checked his rifle, made sure it was ready, and then kept his eyes on the opening. The Apaches would come through it, he was sure. But they'd be easy to pick off when they did.

The firing picked up as the Apaches poured rounds into the cave. It sounded like thunder outside with a screaming of the bullets on the inside.

"Stop it!" screamed Crockett suddenly. "Stop it!" She had her hands over her head to protect herself.

Travis still watched the opening. A shadow passed in front of it, but no one came through. As that happened, he realized that if the Apaches waited until night, there would be no way for him to see them. They could crawl right in and eliminate him and Crockett easily. Or even worse, capture them.

But the Apaches apparently hadn't thought of that. An instant later one of them dived into the chamber. He slipped on the soft, loose sand and when he stopped moving, Travis fired twice. The Indian went down loosely, dead.

"There's another," warned Crockett.

Travis swung his weapon around and pulled the trigger. The Apache fell back into the passageway. A shadow flashed again and Travis fired at it but hit nothing other than stone.

The Apaches began to shoot again. More bullets bounced around the interior of the chamber. Chips of stone were flying as the bullets struck them.

"They keep it up," yelled Crockett over the sounds of the echoes and the firing, "they'll hit us."

Travis said nothing for a moment. As the shooting began to taper again, he said, "Head back into that other chamber."

She turned and began to crawl toward it. Travis still watched the entrance. That was the key. If the Apaches could force that, they would be able to get in and kill them.

But no one appeared there. The firing stopped and Travis was sure they would try to get in again, but no one showed himself. Travis stood up and backed up toward the second passageway.

"You're clear," said Crockett.

Travis didn't look at her. He didn't want anyone getting into the cave without him knowing about it. He was getting worried because it had gotten so quiet out there.

"What are they doing?" asked Crockett.

"I don't know," said Travis. "I hope they're not waiting for dark."

"Why would they do that?"

"Because they could get in here easily then. There would be no way to stop them."

"So what are we going to do?"

That was the question that had Travis stumped. There was only one way out and the Apaches had that one covered. What kept them out of the cave was the same thing that kept Travis and Crockett in. Only one person could move through the passage at a time, and that person was vulnerable to whoever was at the other end.

"Maybe if we go deeper," suggested Crockett.

"And do what?"

"I don't know, but we can't stay here."

Travis shot a glance at her. She was right about that. Staying would mean they would die sometime before morning and probably a lot sooner than that.

"Maybe we can get back in there far enough that they won't be able to find us," he said.

Crockett pushed past him and grabbed one of the torches that was laying in the sand. "We're going to need this."

Travis looked at it and then back up at the main entrance. Still no sign of the Apaches. When Crockett stuck the torch up at him, he slipped a match from his pocket, struck it, and used it to ignite the torch.

"Go first," he said.

Crockett ducked and entered the second tunnel. A moment later Travis followed her. When he came out, he said, "Around behind the gold."

Crockett did as told and Travis followed her. He kept looking back at the entrance to the chamber, but it was wrapped in darkness now. The Apaches, if they knew what was happening, could be sneaking in. Travis didn't think they were.

"I don't see anything," she said.

Travis joined her. The light breeze blowing up from the bowels of the cavern caused the flame to flicker. Travis suddenly realized that it would have to be coming from an opening somewhere. Not necessarily large enough for them to crawl through, but it would certainly be there.

"Over here," she said.

Travis saw that she was standing in front of a rounded opening that looked as if it had been drilled in the stone. It was definitely large enough for them to crawl through.

"Go," he said.

She climbed up and into the tunnel so that she was on her hands and knees with one hand on the stone and one holding the torch. She moved her knee forward, keeping the torch held out in front of her.

Looking back over her shoulder, she called, "Looks to be ten or fifteen feet long."

Travis waited until she was out of the way and then entered the tunnel. He followed her until she stopped and waited as she climbed from the tunnel. He then moved forward and stuck his head out. And couldn't believe what he was seeing.

"My God," he said.

"I didn't think there'd be more," she said. She crouched in front of a chest filled with jewels. This was what she had expected when her father had told her about the gold. She had expected chests.

The whole chamber was guarded by dead Spanish soldiers. They were little more than skeletons now. Or piles of bones. They were sitting around the floor, weapons across their laps as if they were just resting before going back on guard. There were pennants and flags with them, now faded with age.

"Apaches must have brought some of the bodies in to watch the treasure for them."

"Look at this," said Crockett.

There was a wall of silver there. A gigantic wall of silver, the bars as large as those of gold in the other room.

"This couldn't all have come from one wagon train," said Travis.

"If they ambushed one, why not two or three or a dozen?" she said.

As they moved around the huge chamber, they found a row of bodies wrapped in blankets. Some of them were lying with rifles. Old-fashioned rifles. Others had swords and knifes. A few were wrapped in buffalo robes.

"Apache chiefs?" she asked

"Probably," he said.

"Then they'll know about this chamber, too," she said. "We'll have to keep moving.

Together they examined the walls, looking for another way out of the chamber. They found it at the edge of the wall of silver. A triangular-shaped passageway big enough for them to walk through. It sloped down, twisted to the right, and then began to climb again. There was a sound of water dripping from somewhere beyond them.

They came out into another chamber, this one long and narrow. The sound of the water came from it. There was a pool to one side and when Crockett got close to it, they could see that it was very deep. And very clear.

"Can we drink it?" she asked.

Travis dropped to his knees and tasted it. "No reason not to."

Crockett handed him the torch and began to drink. When she finished, she looked up. "And now?"

Travis had noticed that the air was getting fresher again. And warmer. The only problem was that the torch was burning down rapidly. It wouldn't be long before they were left in the dark.

"We'd better get going."

Travis stood and listened, but the only sound was the dripping of the water. Nothing that indicated the Apaches were chasing them.

They moved through the narrow chamber, now climbing upward. Travis stooped as the ceiling came down, but then it raised again and the chamber expanded outward. They turned a corner and in the distance spotted a square of bright sunlight.

"I don't believe it," she said.

"A second entrance," said Travis. "I thought there might be one."

She looked up at the torch. It was about to burn itself out. "I think we've been very lucky," she said.

"All we've done," said Travis, "is get away from the Apaches. We're still stuck out here without horses, food or water,"

"There's water back there," she said.

Travis took a deep breath and looked at her in the fading, flickering light of the torch. He thought about saying something to her, thought about saying something about the danger they'd avoided and then didn't. And then he thought that the gold had saved their lives. Had they not wanted to see it, they would have been with Davis and the others when the Apaches got them. If nothing else, the gold had bought his life for him.

"We'll think of something," she said.

"Once we get out of here," said Travis, "things can only improve."

Chapter Twenty-Six
The Deserts of West Texas
August 26, 1863

The patch of sunlight in the distance didn't seem to be getting any larger. They walked toward it, thinking that it would expand until it was a huge opening in the cave, but that didn't happen. It stayed small and as they approached, Travis realized that it was a tiny hole in the side of the cave.

"We're not going to be able to get out there," said Crockett.

"Sure we are," said Travis. "We might have to dig a little, but we'll get out okay."

The ceiling began to come down again so that they were hunched over. Crockett lowered the torch, and as she did the last of the material around the stick fell to the cave's floor. She looked at it and then back at Travis.

"Doesn't matter," he said. "We can see the way out up there. Just head for it."

She tossed the remains of the torch to the floor. Travis slipped past her. "I'll lead for a while."

They continued on until he was forced to his hands and knees and then to his belly. He pulled himself forward carefully, afraid that he was going to get stuck. The whole tunnel narrowed until he could barely move through it. Finally he got stuck, his holster hanging him up. He slipped to the rear and rolled to his side to unbuckle it. Then he pushed it forward in front of them and held his rifle out in his hand. Now he was able to squeeze through the narrowest part of the tunnel.

Once out of there, he chanced back and saw Crockett down on her stomach, crawling after him. "It's tight but you can make it," he said.

"I know."

He turned and pushed himself forward, but the tiny rectangle of sunlight didn't grow at all. He was close enough to it now to see that it had lighted part of the cave. A few rocks laying on the floor and the stones sticking from the sides were throwing shadows. The opening couldn't be more than a foot square up on the wall. The tunnel turned the opposite way, diving deeper into the mountain. It was almost as if someone had carved a window in the cave wall.

He didn't say anything to Crockett about that. He moved toward it, blinking in the brightness of it. He had thought that it was on the eastern side of the mountain, but with the sun practically shining right in it, it had to be on the west. It was late afternoon now.

As he approached it, he could feel the hot air from outside on the desert drifting toward him. He felt the sweat bead on his forehead.

Again the tunnel began to narrow. He slipped forward, pushing hard against the sides and top of the cave. He stopped no more than a foot from the hole in the wall. He just couldn't make it to that point.

"Why'd you stop?" asked Crockett.

"Can't go any further." He started to push himself back.

"Wait!" snapped Crockett. "What are you doing?"

"Backing up," said Travis. "Move back."

"Wait a minute."

Travis turned his head and tried to look to the rear, but the sides of the cave restricted his movement. He slipped to the rear and then looked at her. "Need to widen the opening a bit so we can get out."

She didn't respond.

Travis pulled his knife and began to scrape at the side of the cave. It had looked like stone, but as he dug into it, he found it to be soft. It crumbled under the digging. He stopped, pushed some of the material to the rear, and began to whittle at the top and right side. Slowly, he worked his way forward until his hand was in a patch of sunlight.

"Getting there," he said, his voice sounding loud and echoing back. Lowering it, he whispered, "Getting there."

He kept at it, the sweat beginning to drip into his eyes, burning them. He ducked his head, wiping his brow on his shoulder and then got back at work, scraping at the cave. He knew he had to be careful. If he broke the knife, they would be stuck. There was no way they would be able to find their way back without light, and the torch was gone.

His arm began to ache and he stopped to rest. He lowered his head because his neck hurt. Lying there on his left side, his knee braced against the wall, his body was twisted into an awkward position.

"What's wrong?"

"Nothing," said Travis. "I'm resting."

"Want me to take over?"

"Just be patient," he said. He then slipped forward and began to work at the sides again.

"The Apaches," she said.

Travis stopped working. He tried to see her, but she was nothing more than a dark shape surrounded by black. "What about them?"

"They're coming."

"How do you know?"

Crockett was silent and the only sounds in the cave were the dripping of the water and a quiet rush of air as the desert wind blew in the hole.

Travis slipped away from it and tried to see or hear something behind her. It stood to reason that the Apaches would infiltrate the cave when no one shot at them. They'd have to be careful, but they'd be moving through it, searching for them. Now Travis didn't know whether to try to finish digging his way out, return to one of the narrow tunnels to make a stand, or to press farther back into the mountain.

"What are you doing?" asked Crockett, her voice hushed.

"Thinking," he snapped. "Thinking."

He turned and began to dig at the wall of the cave, pulling the dirt and rock out in big chunks. He pushed it out of the way, forcing himself to keep working even as his arms turned to lead and his fingers were scraped raw.

He could feel Crockett pressing forward. She had moved up in the tunnel, getting as close to him and the opening as possible. She didn't have to say a word. He could feel her there without hearing her or having to look at her.

Finally she broke the silence. "They're coming."

Travis stopped scraping and pushed himself away from the hole he was creating. Now, over the sound of the dripping water and the rush of desert air into the cave, he could hear the Apaches moving. Quiet sounds, as they felt their way through the darkness of the cave.

With a renewed vigor, he stabbed at the cave's walls, popping bits of the soft limestone away and then scraping to make it even. He forced himself forward, his shoulders jammed against the sides. But he managed to get far enough that he could look out.

"What?" she asked.

Travis slipped back. "We're on the side of the mountain. It slopes down gently. Can't see the front, the river, or any sign of the Apaches."

"Can you get out?"

"Just a moment," he said. With very little effort he thought he could force himself out, but he wasn't quite sure that he wanted to do it yet. Not without being sure what was around them. He'd hate to get out, turn around, and find himself staring into the rifle of one of the Apaches.

He wiped at the sweat on his face with the back of his hand and began to chip away at the last few inches of the cave. Now he was shoving the limestone and dirt out of the cave.

"They're coming," said Crockett. "Get out now."

Travis reached out and tugged a point of rock. It wobbled but didn't come loose. Now he could hear the Apaches. Their voices were echoing along the passage. Maybe they were trying to be quiet or maybe they were trying to frighten Travis into making a panicked mistake.

Using his knife, jamming it into the soft soil of the cave's wall, he popped a chunk of earth free and then yanked at the side. For a moment everything held fast and then, suddenly, it came free. A hole opened in the side large enough to get out.

"That's about it," he said suddenly. He reached back and grabbed the barrel of his rifle, pulling it toward him carefully. The last thing he wanted to have happen was the trigger get hung up on something.

Now he was pushing himself forward. His shoulders scraped on the sides of the cave, but he made it. Suddenly his head and shoulders were outside the cave. He turned slightly, looked up the mountain, and saw nothing except clouds building in the west. The mountainside was empty.

Pushing, he rolled out onto the desert. He scrambled around, the rifle in his hands, but spotted no one. Down the mountain was a wide valley. There were clumps of Joshua trees, cactus, yucca plants, and thick grass. There was no movement anywhere except for a couple of birds in the sky windmilling on the currents.

Crockett shoved herself up and reached out toward him. "Help me."

Travis looked down and then grabbed her hand. He pulled her up, hauling her out of the cave in a single, fluid motion. She fell to the ground.

"They're coming," she said. "They're behind me."

Now, from the cave, he could hear the pursuit. The Apaches were no longer worried about stealth. They were running forward, the light from the hole guiding them.

"Come on," said Travis. He grabbed her hand and pulled her up the slope, toward a distant outcropping of rock.

As they reached it, the first of the Apaches poked his head out the hole. He dropped out of sight quickly. Travis dropped to the ground and then drew his revolver from his holster. "Here. Hang onto that."

He cocked the rifle and aimed at the hole, waiting. He knew that the instant he pulled the trigger he would alert the rest of the Apaches. They had gotten out of the cave, had gotten away from the massacre on the other side of the mountain, but it was going to do them no good.

The Apache didn't peek out again. He leaped up and out, rolling away. Travis fired, but the round hit the ground, kicking up a cloud of dust and dirt. The Indian whooped, jumped to his feet, and began running at him. Travis aimed and fired. The bullet struck home, knocking the man from his feet.

But now others were coming out. They were shouting and shooting. Bullets snapped through the air overhead. One hit a rock and tumbled off with a ricochetting noise.

Travis worked the lever, fired, and then swung around. Two more Indians were running at him, both shooting as they ran. He felt chips of stone, kicked up by the bullets, cut his face.

Now Crockett was shooting. He'd wanted her to save the bullets in the pistol for them, but she didn't. She aimed at the closest of the Apaches. The bullet slammed into his face and knocked him from his feet.

Travis fired at the last of the men out there. Once, twice, three times, finally dropping the Apache. He tried to get to his feet, but Travis shot him again.

Then, suddenly, it was quiet. The last echoes of the firing died and the only sounds were the distant calls of birds and a rustling of the wind through the thick prairie grasses.

Travis scrambled to reload his weapon. He then took the pistol and replaced the rounds. Finished, he surveyed the mountainside. They couldn't go down. That was where the Apaches were. He didn't know if there were others in the cave waiting for them to come back, or if all those who had followed had climbed out.

"What?" asked Crockett. It sounded as if she had sprinted up the mountain toward him.

Travis got to his feet and jerked her up. He pointed at the top of the mountain. "There," he said.

"Why?"

"Because it's the only direction open to us."

She began to climb, running where she could. Travis kept looking back, glancing over his shoulder, but no more Apaches appeared there. That began to bother him. Someone should be appearing.

Crockett reached the summit and dropped to the ground. She turned to look at him. Sweat had soaked her hair and her blouse. Her complexion was pale.

Travis knelt beside her, the breath rasping in his throat. He looked down the mountain toward the cave, but the Apaches had not reappeared. Then, looking down to the west, on the floor of the valley, Travis spotted riders. At first it was the cloud of dust kicked up by the horses that he saw. He turned and studied them. They were little more than dark specks against the tans of the desert.

"Apaches?" she asked.

Travis shrugged. "I don't know. Could be."

"They know we're here?"

"They're not coming this way," he said. "Echoing of the shots might have confused them."

A second group of riders appeared. They rode toward the first, coming down on them from over a far rise. Firing erupted and Travis understood.

"That's the army,' he said, his voice rising in excitement.

"You sure?"

Before he could respond, the first group stopped and dismounted. They spread out, forming a skirmish line, a couple of men remaining behind to hold the reins of the horses.

"What do you plan to do?" asked Crockett.

Travis glanced at her and then turned his attention back to the men far below. He watched as clouds of smoke billowed out, reaching for the onrushing enemy. It was a scene that he had witnessed in a dozen battles back east.

The wall of lead slammed into the Apaches, knocking a couple of them from their horses. As the sound from the first volley reached them, there was a second and a third. That broke the Indian attack. The survivors whirled, riding back up the slope.

"What are we going to do?" asked Crockett again.

"Hurry down there," said Travis, "and join up with the soldiers."

"You mean that we made it?" she asked, surprised.

"I mean that it looks as if we're going to get out of here alive," he said.

Chapter Twenty-Seven
Hammetsville, Texas
September 12, 1863

"We're going to have to do something," said Emma Crockett. "People are beginning to talk."

Travis sat at the table in her small cabin sipping a cup of coffee. She stood near the fireplace. He asked, "Does that bother you? That they're talking?"

"No, not really. It did when they called my father crazy because he was looking for the Spanish gold, but it doesn't bother me now. Not after all we've done and seen."

"Especially since you're going to be a very rich lady in a couple of months." He grinned and set the cup down. "Very rich."

She moved from the fireplace to the table and sat down. She looked right into Travis's eyes. "There are ways of stopping the talk."

"Like me moving into the hotel, or returning to the east?" he asked.

"No," she said. "That wouldn't stop the talk but make it louder."

Travis realized that all the gold and silver in the cave along with his leaving would not stop the talk. It would only make the tongues wag faster. And he knew what the only sure cure for the wagging tongues would be. A subject that had never come up between them.

Staring at her, Travis asked, "This what you want?"

She nodded slowly, but was looking down at the table as if afraid to face him. "I never thought we'd get out of that cave," she said. "I still think about that cave. Dream about it."

Travis knew what she was saying. He'd thought the same thing, and once they were out, he thought they'd never live to reach El Paso. But the company from the Texas Cavalry had come along, chased away the Apaches, and then escorted them into the city. The escort was large enough that the Apaches, if they had been around, hadn't bothered it. That was the thing about the Indians. They never attacked unless they felt the odds were on their side.

But that was just talk to disguise what was really on her mind. They had been over that end of the rescue a hundred times, and they had talked about how it had been too bad that the cavalry hadn't arrived a couple of hours earlier. They had been there to save Travis and Crockett but not Davis and the others.

Travis decided that he didn't want to think about Davis and the others, about the gold they couldn't get at for the moment, and everything else that went with it. Instead he decided that he'd rather think about Emma Crockett and what life would be like with only memories of her.

"We can afford to do anything you want," he said. "Maybe not right this minute but in the very near future."

"Then," she said quietly, "what I'd really like to do is go back, get a bar or two of the gold, sell it, and travel to New Orleans to get married."

"There's a war on and the Union has New Orleans," he said.

"I don't care about the war."

Travis got up and walked over to the bed they had been sharing for the last few weeks. He reached under the mattress and pulled out a small leather bag. He returned to the table, opened the bag, and spilled the contents on the table.

"I didn't see you take those."

"You were searching for a way out," said Travis. "I thought that if we got out, that would keep us in food and clothes until we could get back for some of the gold."

"You never said a word."

"One of those could be mounted into a ring and the others used for a honeymoon."

She glanced up at him and said, "I thought you'd never ask."

"I take that as a yes?"

"Yes," she said. "Of course." She reached up and began unbuttoning her blouse. She grinned shyly, as if it was the first time she had done that for him.

Travis stood and moved to the bed, pulling the cover down. He turned and waited for her to join him. "Tomorrow," he said, "We'll leave for New Orleans."

Still grinning, she said, "Not too early."

"No," he agreed. "Not too early."